Heartland™

Thicker Than Water

The pretty grey pony pricked his ears and whinnied. Jo raced down the aisle and flung her arms round his neck. "Hey, boy. How are you?" she said, kissing him several times on his soft nose. He nuzzled her.

"I think he's pleased to see you," Amy said.

"Not as much as I am to see him," Jo said. She hugged him hard. "He's my best friend and I don't care what Mom says, I'm never ever going to let him go."

Amy felt a chill of apprehension run through her at Jo's words. She hoped that she was going to be able to cure Feather. But what if she couldn't? What would Jo do then?

Read all the books about Heartland:

www.scholastic.co.uk/zone

Heartland™

Thicker Than Water

Lauren Brooke

■SCHOLASTIC

With special thanks to Linda Chapman

For Elaine

Scholastic Children's Books,
Euston House, 24 Eversholt Street,
London NW1 1DB, UK
A division of Scholastic Ltd
London ~ New York ~ Toronto ~ Sydney ~ Auckland
Mexico City ~ New Delhi ~ Hong Kong

First published in the UK by Scholastic Ltd, 2002
Series created by Working Partners Ltd

Copyright © Working Partners Ltd, 2002

Heartland is a trademark of Working Partners Ltd.

10 digit ISBN 0 439 99453 5
13 digit ISBN 978 0439 99453 8

Typeset by TW Typesetting, Midsomer Norton, Somerset
Printed and bound in Denmark by Nørhaven Paperback A/S, Viborg

12 14 16 18 20 19 17 15 13

The right of Lauren Brooke to be identified as the author of this work has
been asserted by her in accordance with the Copyright, Designs and
Patents Act, 1988.

Chapter One

The Appaloosa filly snorted and threw her head high. Her eyes rolled. Every muscle in her body was tense.

"Easy now, Rosie," fifteen-year-old Amy Fleming murmured. Her right hand moved the skin on the horse's neck in light circles. With each circle she made, she breathed out softly. In her left hand she held a halter. From outside the stall came the everyday sounds of the busy boarding stables where Rosie was kept. Stable-hands were calling to each other, horses were stamping their hooves and snorting, visitors were walking up and down the barn aisles, but Amy barely heard any of it. Her attention was riveted on the frightened filly.

"Be careful, Amy," Lou said from the stall door, where she was standing with Sheri Hegland, Rosie's owner.

Amy heard the anxiety in her sister's voice. She nodded,

but her determined grey eyes remained focused on the horse. "It's OK, girl," she whispered. "I'm not going to hurt you. I'm here to help."

"She's been like this ever since I bought her," Sheri said. "She just freaks every time I try to halter her. If you can't cure her, I don't know what I'm going to do."

"We'll do our best," Lou said.

"It must feel good – helping horses that have problems or have been abused," Sheri said. "I bet it gives you an amazing buzz."

Amy heard Lou clear her throat rather awkwardly. "Actually, I don't really have much to do with the treatment of the horses myself. It's Amy and our stable-hand, Ty, who work with the horses. I just help with the business side of things."

Not *just*, Amy corrected Lou in her mind. Heartland – the equine sanctuary founded by their mother – couldn't survive without someone managing the business side of things as well.

Amy focused on the filly again. Rosie's head had lowered and she seemed to have relaxed slightly. Amy moved her hand towards the horse's ears, but as soon as she did so, Rosie stiffened again. Moving her hand back, Amy contented herself on working some more on Rosie's neck. It looked like getting the halter on the filly was going to be a long, slow process – but if she had to take her time, then that was what she would do.

Ten minutes later, Amy's fingers had finally reached the top of Rosie's neck. As her hand inched towards the filly's ears, she noticed a long scar running down the outside of the left one. What had caused it? An accident? Ill-treatment?

"Do you know what might have caused this scar?" Amy asked Sheri.

"I'm afraid not," Sheri answered her. "I don't know that much about Rosie's history. I bought her as an unbroken three-year-old at a horse sale in Maryland. The guy selling her said he hadn't done anything with her apart from halter-training her. He said she was quiet, but when I tried to halter her the next day she went crazy, rearing up and banging her head on the stall partition."

"Hmm." Amy looked thoughtful. Looking at the scar on Rosie's ear, Amy felt sure that it had something to do with the way the filly was behaving. She scanned Rosie's face. Her head had lowered again and she looked almost relaxed. It was time to get the halter on. Tightening her grip on it, Amy slipped it over the filly's nose.

Rosie immediately jerked her head up, but Amy was too quick for her. Flipping the headpiece behind the Appaloosa's ears, she fastened the buckle.

"Whoa, there," she soothed.

Rosie's muscles trembled, but at the touch of Amy's hand on her neck she slowly calmed down.

"Well done, Amy," Lou said in relief.

"She'll be OK, now," Sheri said quickly. "It's just getting the halter on that causes it. That's why I didn't realize the problem until I got her home — she had the halter on all the time at the sale, and I didn't think to check to see if she'd let me take it on and off. If you hang on to her, I'll go fetch her travel wraps."

As Sheri hurried away down the barn aisle, Amy reached round to tighten the scrunchie that was securing her light-brown hair in a long pony-tail. "Looks like we've got some work to do with you, girl," she said, scratching the Appaloosa affectionately on the neck.

Rosie snorted softly, calm now.

Lou, so different-looking from Amy with her short golden hair, came into the stall. "I almost thought you weren't going to be able to get that halter on. You were so patient with her."

Hearing the admiration in her sister's voice, Amy shrugged. "It's just experience. Mom taught me everything before —" she struggled for a moment with the words — "before she died." It was almost eight months since their mom, Marion, had been killed in a road accident. The intense grief that Amy had felt straight after the accident had diminished, but she carried with her a deep sense of loss that she knew would never fade.

Lou sighed. "I wish I were half as good with horses as you."

There was a wistful note in her sister's voice that made Amy look at her in surprise. Since moving from Manhattan to Heartland to live, Lou had shied away from getting involved with the horses – all apart from Sugarfoot, a little Shetland. This was the first time that Amy had heard Lou suggest that she would like things to be different.

"But you could be," Amy said to her. "You just need to spend more time with them. If you wanted, I could teach you everything Mom taught me."

"Really?" For a moment, Lou looked almost tempted. "You mean I could learn how to heal them like you do?"

"Sure," Amy said. She imagined Lou helping her, just as she herself had once helped their mom. "It would be cool, Lou." She looked at her sister's face and saw a sudden look of excitement there. "Why not?"

Just then Sheri came to the doorway. "Here are the wraps and her tail bandage. Shall I put them on?"

Sheri's appearance shattered the intimacy of the moment. In the blink of an eye, the eagerness left Lou's face and her expression became cool and controlled once more.

"Thanks, Sheri," she replied briskly. "I'll go and lower the ramp on the trailer. When Rosie's ready, bring her round to the parking lot."

"But Lou...?" Amy protested.

Lou's eyes seemed to slip away from hers. "Maybe it's better if I just stick to what I know best," she said quietly, and with that she walked off.

Sheri looked a bit confused. "Sorry – did I interrupt something?" she asked, watching Lou go.

"It's OK," Amy replied. She stared after Lou for a moment and then brought her mind back to the job in hand. "Let's get Rosie ready."

Taking the tail bandage from Sheri, she began to wrap it around Rosie's tail.

If only Lou would help with the horses more, Amy thought, as Sheri began to put the leg protectors on. *Then maybe we'd get on better. We might even go out riding together...*

Amy brushed aside the thoughts. It was hardly likely. After all, Lou hadn't ridden for over twelve years.

She tied up the bandage and saw that Sheri had just put on the last leg wrap and was straightening up. Amy fixed a smile on her face. "OK," she said, patting Rosie's hindquarters. "Looks like she's ready to go."

The Heartland trailer was in the large parking lot. Tall Oaks, the boarding barn where Rosie was stabled, had over seventy stalls. The paddocks stretched out in all directions around the parking lot, and to the left were three training rings.

Rosie loaded easily into the trailer. Apart from her head-shyness, she didn't seem to be a particularly nervous horse. Quiet and reserved maybe, Amy thought as she tied her up, but not nervous.

"We'll give you a ring tonight and let you know how she's settling in," Lou told Sheri as they fastened the bolts holding the ramp up. "And of course, feel free to visit any time you want."

"Thanks," Sheri said. "I sure hope you can help her." She went round to the jockey door and gave Rosie a last pat. "You be good now, girl."

Rosie whickered in reply.

Lou fastened the door and turned to Amy. "I just want to take some of our brochures to the office," she said. "Maybe we'll get some more business from here."

Amy nodded. Having brochures advertising Heartland's services had been Lou's idea. She dropped them off wherever she could – tack stores, grain merchants, boarding barns like this one. So far the leaflets had generated a fair bit of work and Amy, who had originally been opposed to the idea, was having to admit that maybe they had been a good move after all. Just like Lou's idea of having a fund-raising barn dance, and the open day to show off the techniques that Heartland used to heal horses.

But then not all of Lou's ideas had worked, Amy thought. Sometimes her sister got so caught up in making money that she seemed to forget that Heartland was more than just a business – it was about horses, living, breathing horses.

Amy glanced at her watch. How long was Lou going to be? She wandered up the yard, past the barns, towards the three training rings. There was just one rider out – a girl, younger than Amy, who was trotting a rose-grey Arabian pony around the ring. The pony looked tense and as Amy approached, he slowed to a stop. Tossing his head, he tried to plunge towards the gate.

But the girl was clearly a good rider. Sitting deep in her saddle, she urged him on.

Amy recognized her. Her name was Jo-Ann Newhart and she was at the elementary school that Amy had gone to. She must be in about sixth grade now, Amy thought, watching as the younger girl refused to let her pony get away with napping to the gate.

"Please be careful, honey," a woman watching at the fence called out to the girl. "I think you ought to bring him in. He really doesn't look too happy."

"He's fine, Mom!" Jo-Ann said swiftly. "Go on, Feather!" she exclaimed as the grey pony stopped again. Although her riding position was good, her shoulders looked bunched-up and tense. She kicked Feather on, glancing round at her mom as she did so.

The pony seemed determined not to move. Shaking his head, he began to back up. Jo-Ann clicked her tongue and kicked his sides but he kept going backwards. Jo-Ann turned him in a circle and he stopped dead.

"OK, that's enough," Mrs Newhart said, her voice high and nervous. "I want you to bring him in now, Jo-Ann."

"No," Jo-Ann said and Amy thought she heard a note of desperation in the younger girl's voice. Bringing her whip down, Jo-Ann smacked Feather on his shoulder. Amy saw the pony sink down on his hocks.

"Watch out!" she gasped instinctively, but it was too late. Feather had reared into the air.

Mrs Newhart screamed as Jo-Ann threw herself forward on Feather's neck just as he came down.

"Turn him in a circle, Jo!" Amy shouted above the sound of Mrs Newhart's screams. She scrambled over the gate, wondering wildly if she could somehow grab the pony's reins before he went up again. But before she could reach him, Jo had done what Amy had said. Throwing her weight to one side, she pulled the pony's head and neck round in as tight a circle as possible. Thrown off balance, there was no way that Feather could rear up again.

"Are you OK?" Amy demanded, grabbing the pony's reins before he decided to try anything else.

Jo's face was white with shock, but she nodded at Amy. "I'm ... I'm fine."

"Jo-Ann! Please! Get off that animal right now!"

Amy and Jo glanced round. A shocked-looking Mrs Newhart was fumbling with the gate.

"I'm OK, Mom," Jo protested.

"Now, Jo-Ann!"

Looking very reluctant, Jo threw one leg over the saddle and slid off Feather's back. Mrs Newhart got the gate open and came running across the ring towards her. "That's the last straw," she said, her voice shaking. "That pony's dangerous. Your uncle should never have bought him for you!"

"It's fine, Mom. I'm all right," Jo insisted.

"Yes, this time," her mom replied. "But what about when it happens again?" She shook her head. "I'm sorry, honey. I'm going to get rid of him. I can't have you risking yourself like this."

"Mom!" Jo exclaimed.

Mrs Newhart looked like she was about to take Feather's reins off Jo but then she seemed to think better of it. She suddenly seemed to notice Amy. "Thanks for helping," she said quickly. "Can you give Jo-Ann a hand putting Feather back in the barn? I don't think she should lead him on her own." It was obvious that she thought Amy worked at Tall Oaks.

Amy didn't bother to tell her that she didn't. "Sure," she said, looking sympathetically at Jo.

"I don't need any help, thank you," Jo said angrily. Grabbing Feather's reins, she began to march towards the gate, but before she went Amy caught a glimpse of the tears welling up in her hazel eyes.

"I'm going to wait in the car," Mrs Newhart called after her. "I expect you to join me in five minutes. Is that clear?"

Jo nodded briefly and led Feather out of the ring.

Amy hurried after her. "Are you OK?"

Jo stopped dead. "OK?" she exclaimed. "How can I be OK? My mom's going to sell Feather!" Her angry words hung in the air, then a look of contrition came on to her face. "Sorry," she said. "I didn't mean to shout. It's not your fault — it's Mom's." She swallowed and led Feather on again.

Amy felt desperately sorry for her. "Your mom's just worried, Jo," she said, following her. "Rearers are dangerous

— if Feather fell over on you he could break your back. Maybe it's for the best if you get another pony."

"You don't understand," Jo said, one hand gripping Feather's mane. "I won't get another one. Mom didn't want me to have Feather in the first place. My uncle bought him for me and now this has happened, Mom will never let me have another! She hates horses — she always has."

Amy was shocked.

"It's so unfair," Jo went on, as she led Feather into his stall. "Feather's not dangerous. I mean, he has his crazy days — usually when Mom happens to be watching — but he's only reared a couple of times before." Feather rubbed his grey head against her chest and snorted happily.

Amy frowned. Her own mom had always said that you could analyse a horse's personality by looking at its face, and looking at Feather, she thought that the shape of his face backed up what Jo had said. He had large, almond-shaped eyes — normally the sign of a gentle, soft-natured horse. He was an Arabian and his dished face, fluted ears and complex, wrinkled chin suggested that he was likely to be an extremely sensitive, cooperative character. Feather sure didn't look mean, stubborn or resistant.

"You say he's only reared a couple of times?" she said.

Jo nodded. "Yes. Like I said, most of the time he's perfect."

Amy frowned and, after offering her hand to the pony to sniff, she started to feel along his back and neck with her hands. "Maybe he's sore somewhere," she said to Jo.

Suddenly, a light seem to come on in the younger girl's eyes.

"Amy!" she said. "You know all about horses with problems, don't you? Well, can't you help me? Mom would have to let me keep him if you said you could cure him. We could bring him to Heartland until he's better and then—"

"Whoa!" Amy interrupted her. "Even if Feather comes to Heartland, there's no guarantee that we can help him. Rearers are dangerous." She saw Jo's face fall. "But I guess there is a chance that we could help," she said quickly. "If there's a genuine reason for him rearing – like pain – then maybe we can cure him, particularly seeing as his rearing hasn't become an established habit."

"Oh, please say you'll try!" Jo begged her.

Amy looked at her pleading eyes. "OK," she said. "I'll try."

"Thank you!" Jo gasped. "Oh," she said suddenly. "But what about Mom? She wants to sell him."

"Let's get my sister," Amy said quickly. "She's really good at persuading people. Maybe if she talked to your mom then we might get her to let Feather come to Heartland."

She jogged back to the trailer.

Lou was waiting there. "I was just beginning to get worried about you," she said.

"Lou, I need to talk to you." Seeing Mrs Newhart sitting in a car nearby, Amy pulled Lou round the far side of the trailer and explained about Feather.

"I think we could help him – at least, I'd like to give it a try," she said. "We've got a free stall now that Gallant Prince has gone."

Lou looked concerned.

"Feather's only reared a couple of times," Amy went on. "And there might be a genuine reason for his behaviour – pain or fear. If we take that away then his rearing should stop."

Lou still looked worried. "But rearing is one of the hardest things to treat. I'm sure I remember Mom once saying that there's no safe way to deal with a rearing horse."

"I'll be careful," Amy said. "I've got to at least try to help."

Lou hesitated for a moment. "OK," she said at last, although her eyes were reluctant. "Let's go and get him."

Amy took a deep breath. "There's a bit of a problem."

Lou looked at her questioningly.

"Jo's mom," Amy admitted.

To Amy's relief, Lou agreed to help her persuade Mrs Newhart to allow Feather to go to Heartland.

"I'm sure there's a chance we can help him," Lou said to Mrs Newhart, as she and Amy explained Jo's idea. "Amy and Ty are both very experienced in dealing with problem horses."

"And we have dealt with rearers before," Amy said.

"Please say yes," Jo begged her mom. "It'll be perfect. Heartland's close to our house and I'll be able to see him regularly."

Mrs Newhart looked worried. "I'm really not sure."

"Even if you just let us have him for a few weeks," Lou said. "Let's see if we can help him."

"Please, Mom," Jo said. "You just can't sell him without giving him a second chance."

"All right," Mrs Newhart agreed reluctantly. "He can go to Heartland for one month." Jo's face lit up. "But if he isn't cured within that time, then we are selling him," she added firmly. "And you're not to ride him until I'm sure he's safe, Jo."

"I won't," Jo promised. She hugged her mom. "Thanks, Mom."

Amy felt a mixture of relief and anxiety. One month wasn't long. What if they couldn't help him in that time?

"You need to tell me everything you know about his past," she said to Jo, as they went to Feather's stall to get him ready to travel. "It might help me work out what's making him play up. Has he been moved around a lot? Has he had lots of owners? Things like that can often unsettle a horse."

"But that hasn't happened to Feather," Jo said. "My uncle bought him from a family he knew in Maryland. They'd had him for five years and were only selling him because the youngest daughter had outgrown him. They'd bought him from his breeder when he was four years old. She showed him in conformation classes."

Amy frowned. "So there's never been any hint of bad behaviour before?"

"No," Jo said. "And, like I told you, most of the time he's

14

really good with me. It's just sometimes that he goes crazy." She looked at Amy. "You will be able to help him, won't you?" she said anxiously.

"I'll try my best," Amy promised her. "I really will."

Feather loaded easily into the trailer. He sniffed noses with Rosie and then nuzzled Jo. "I'll come and visit you tomorrow, baby," she promised, kissing his muzzle. Her voice dropped to a whisper. "I love you."

Amy smiled. Because Jo was several years younger than her, she hadn't really seen much of her when they were both at the same school. But although she had only met her for a short time that day, already she was already beginning to like her.

I just hope I can help her and Feather, she thought, as Jo jumped out of the trailer, her dark-red hair bouncing on her shoulders.

"I'll see you tomorrow, Amy," Jo called.

"Yeah, see you!" Amy smiled. She got into the pick-up beside Lou.

Lou raised her eyebrows as Amy shut the door. "Now, you're sure there aren't any other horses that you want us to squeeze in while we're at it?" she teased.

"Well, there is some space in the tack compartment," Amy said, pretending to consider Lou's question seriously. "I suppose I could always go and see if I can find a little pony." She put her hand on the door handle.

Lou quickly started the engine. "Too late!" she said, putting her foot down on the gas pedal and smiling. "Which is probably just as well. I'm already thinking of what Ty will say when we get back!"

Amy grinned. That was true. What would Ty say when they unloaded not one horse, but two!

Chapter Two

"Amy!" Ty exclaimed as Amy lowered the trailer ramp to the ground. "There's another horse in there!"

Amy pretended astonishment. "Gee!" she said, looking at him innocently. "How did that get in there?"

Ty shook his head at her, a smile already tugging at the corners of his sensitive, determined mouth. "OK – explain."

"He reared with his owner, Jo, while I was watching and her mom wanted to sell him," Amy said. She saw Ty's face start to crease into a frown. "I had to help."

"But a rearer..." Ty began, raking a hand through his dark hair.

"I know they're difficult, but he's only reared a couple of times before," Amy said. "Just take a look at him, Ty," she said, seeing the concern in Ty's eyes. "He's not mean, you can see he's not."

Ty's green eyes scanned her face and Amy felt her stomach turn a familiar somersault. She and Ty weren't exactly dating, but at Christmas-time he had kissed her – and sometimes, all it took was one look to bring the memory of that moment flooding back.

"I'll ... I'll get him out," she said hastily, horribly aware of the blood that had flamed into her cheeks. "Then you can see what you think."

Ducking her head to hide her embarrassment, she went round to the jockey door. Rosie, the Appaloosa, was standing quietly, her head lowered, her eyes half-closed. Giving her a quick pat, Amy untied Feather's lead-rope and backed him out of the trailer.

The grey Arabian pony pranced out, his head high. As soon as his hooves hit the gravel, he swung round, his eyes darting across to the turn-out paddocks on either side of Heartland's long driveway and then round to the old brick stable-block that stood at a right-angle to the white, weather-boarded farmhouse.

With a snort, Feather lifted his front leg and began to paw at the gravel with a quick, sharp movement of his hoof.

"Steady, fella," Ty said, stroking him. "He seems spirited," he commented. "Not a novice's pony."

Amy nodded. "Yeah, but Jo's a good rider. She's got a great seat – she stayed on him no problem when he went up in the air." She glanced at Ty. He was studying the pony's fine-boned face. "So, what do you reckon?" she said.

"Sensitive, gentle," Ty said, his eyes scanning Feather's delicate ears, large eyes and small muzzle. "The sort of horse that might panic if he's scared or in pain." He turned and nodded. "Yeah — you did the right thing. Maybe there is a problem with him that we can solve. He sure doesn't look mean."

Amy felt a rush of relief. It was good to have Ty agree with her. He'd been working at Heartland since he was fifteen — just at weekends and in vacations at first, but when he was sixteen he'd left school and her mom had offered him a full-time job. Marion had always said that he was a natural with horses.

"First thing we need to do," Ty went on, "is to get Scott to check him over to see if he's carrying an injury that might be making him rear."

Amy nodded. Scott Trewin was the local equine vet. "And if there's no injury…"

"…we take it from there," Ty finished.

They smiled at each other and Amy felt a glow of happiness surge through her. She and Ty worked so well together, it was like they could read each other's thoughts.

"Here," Ty said, holding out his hand. "I'll put him away in Gallant Prince's old stall, if you unload the filly. I've bedded down the stable next to Jake's for her."

"Thanks," Amy said, handing the lead-rope over.

She ducked under the breast bar of the trailer and began to untie Rosie. The gentle Appaloosa rubbed her head against Amy's arm.

"You're a sweet girl, aren't you," Amy murmured, stroking Rosie's chestnut-and-white flecked neck. "Come on, let's put you in your new stall." With a slight toss of her head, Rosie backed obediently out of the trailer and followed Amy up the yard.

Amy was just pushing the bolt across the white-painted stable door when she heard a clatter of hooves. She looked round. Ben Stillman, Heartland's newest stable-hand, was riding his chestnut jumper, Red, in from the trails.

"Hi, there!" he greeted her. "Is that the new horse?" He nodded to Rosie who was rubbing the side of the head along the top of the half-door.

Amy nodded. "One of them." She saw Ben's enquiring look and shook her head. "It's a long story, but there's another in the back barn, in Prince's old stall."

Ben raised his eyebrows. "I'll untack Red and you can tell me all about it."

Amy clipped Rosie's lead-rope to the hook outside the stall door and followed Ben to Red's stall, two doors down. Ben had come to work at Heartland a few months ago. Although it had taken a while for him to settle in, he was now definitely part of Heartland's extended family.

"So, come on? What's the story?" Ben said as Amy appeared in the doorway.

Amy bent down and began to help take off Red's brushing boots. As she did so, she told Ben all about Jo and Feather.

"I had to say we'd help," she finished.

"Course you did," Ben said, his eyes concerned. "Poor kid – I bet she was really upset."

Amy nodded. "I just hope we can cure him."

"If anyone can, it's you and Ty," Ben said.

Amy felt a warm glow. "Thanks," she said, smiling at him. She patted Red. "How was he today?"

"Jumping out of his skin," Ben said. "There's an indoor training show on at Willow Creek on Sunday that I think I might go to. Do you want to come? They've got junior jumpers – you could enter Sundance."

"Yeah!" Amy said immediately. Sundance, her pony, was a brilliant jumper. He'd won Large Pony Champion several times and, for a while now, Amy had been wanting to try him in the jumper division, but she was always so busy at Heartland, and there was never usually anyone free to take her to shows.

"I bet he'll storm the class," Ben said.

"I'll need to get some practice in," Amy said, quickly trying to work out when she would have the time. Being February, the nights still closed in really early. But maybe, if she rode him before school, she could...

"Oh," she said suddenly, as a thought struck her. "When did you say the show was?"

"Sunday."

Amy's heart sank. "Then it's no good, I can't go."

"Why not?" Ben asked.

"My —" Amy's throat felt suddenly dry as she struggled over the word — "my father's visiting at the weekend."

Ben's eyes leaped to her face. "Your father?" he echoed.

"Lou arranged it," Amy said. She fought down a faint flicker of excitement. She was not going to feel any emotion over a visit from the man who had deserted her, Lou and their mom over twelve years ago. After all, he'd never even tried to get in touch until last year. She corrected herself, as a memory of a letter sent five years ago forced its way into her mind. In the letter he had begged her mom for a reconciliation. *But he didn't really try*, Amy thought angrily. *He could have written again*.

A defiant look lit up her grey eyes. "Maybe I will come after all," she declared. "I can always see him when I get back in the evening." She tilted her chin. "In fact, the less time I spend with him the better."

"But you haven't seen him for twelve years, Amy," Ben protested.

"So?" Amy shrugged, doing her best to ignore the little voice in her mind that screamed, *What do you mean — so? He's your father!* "It doesn't mean I have to spend time with him now. No, I'll come to the show with you."

"Oh, no, you won't," Ben said. "I wouldn't have asked you if I'd known your dad was visiting." Amy opened her mouth to object but he cut in before she could speak. "Come on, Amy. More than anyone, I know how important it is to sort things out with your parents — even if you don't want to."

"But..." Amy began.

Ben shook his head. "You know I missed out on a whole lot by cutting my mom out of my life for six years. Give your dad a chance. If you don't, you'll be the one that loses out."

Amy looked at him mutinously, but, deep down, she knew he was right. And anyway, there was Lou to think about, too. This visit meant an awful lot to her — for years she'd lived in hope of their father returning. She would go crazy if Amy took off to a show the very weekend their father was here. "OK," she sighed. "I guess I can go to the next show with you?"

Ben smiled at her. "Sure you can." Slinging Red's saddle and bridle over his arm, he walked to the door. "It's the best thing to do, Amy. You know it is."

"Yeah, right," Amy muttered.

Kicking out at a few loose stones, she walked up the yard to the back barn to find Ty.

If only her dad wasn't coming to visit. She, Lou and Grandpa had their own life without him. Why couldn't he just stay in Australia with his new wife, Helena, and their child?

As she walked through the barn door, several horses whinnied. Despite feeling cranky, Amy couldn't help but smile. That was the best thing about horses. You just couldn't stay in a bad mood when you were around them.

She stopped briefly at each of the stalls that lined the wide concrete aisle, giving out pats and horse cookies.

"Hey there," Ty said, looking out over Feather's door, as she reached Sugarfoot's stall.

"Hi," Amy said, as the little Shetland poked his nose up to the stall door and nuzzled her hands for cookies, his dark eyes peeking out cheekily from under his thick flaxen forelock.

Ty seemed to hear the faint sigh in her voice. He frowned. "What's wrong?"

"Nothing," Amy muttered. She fed Sugarfoot a final cookie and went into Feather's stall.

Ty's frown deepened. "Something's the matter. What's up?"

Amy saw the concern in his eyes and suddenly everything came rushing out. "It's Daddy's visit. I don't want him to come here, Ty. I don't want to see him!"

Ty walked over. "Hey," he said softly, putting his hand on her shoulder. "I know it's going to be tough, but think of it this way – by meeting him you can finally come to terms with the past."

Amy lifted her eyes to his.

"After all, you only have to do it the once," Ty went on. "If you don't like him then you don't have to see him again."

"I suppose," Amy grimaced. "I just wish I didn't have to meet him even once."

"I don't think you can avoid that," Ty said, drawing her close. "Come on. It'll be OK."

Amy felt his head lowering towards hers, but just as she

was sure he was about to kiss her, they heard the sound of Ben whistling as he walked into the barn. They sprang apart guiltily. No one, apart from Soraya, Amy's best friend, had any idea that they were more than just good friends. And that was the way Amy wanted to keep it. Until they had decided exactly where their new relationship was going, she wanted as few people as possible to know. It was less complicated that way.

"Hi," Ben called, coming over to the stall. "So this is the new pony, then?" he said, looking at Feather, who was pulling quickly and nervously at his hay net.

"Yes," Amy said, hoping he wouldn't notice her confusion.

"Nice-looking," Ben commented. "Polish bloodlines, I'd say by the look of him." Ben had spent most of the last six years of his life on his aunt's Arabian stud farm and he knew far more than Amy did about Arabians. "Do you know anything about his history?"

"A bit," Amy said.

"So what made him go up today?" Ben mused.

"That's what we've got to find out," Ty said. "Then we can help him."

Amy looked at the pretty grey pony with the chestnut flecks in his coat and the silvery mane and tail. Ty was right. Until they found the reason for his behaviour they wouldn't be able to help. And she desperately wanted to help him — as much as for his own sake as for Jo's.

* * *

25

At the end of the day, after the horses had been fed, the stalls skipped out and the water-buckets checked, Amy waved Ty and Ben off and walked wearily down to the house.

She walked into the warm kitchen. A beef stew was bubbling on the stove and Lou was leaning against the sink talking on the phone. Amy shrugged off her barn-jacket and slung it over the back of one of the chairs. Lou automatically reached out and hooked it on to the new coat rail that she had recently fixed to the back of the kitchen door.

"OK, I better go," she said into the phone. "See you tomorrow."

"Is it Scott?" Amy mouthed to Lou.

Lou nodded.

"Can I speak to him?" Amy said.

Lou nodded again. "Amy's here, Scott. She wants a word." There was a pause and then, "Yeah, me too," Lou murmured softly into the phone.

Amy grinned. Scott and Lou had started dating a few months back and, judging by the sappy look in her sister's blue eyes, things still seemed to be going well.

Seeing her grin, Lou blushed and hurriedly held out the phone.

"Hi, Scott," Amy said.

"Amy!" Scott's warm voice greeted her. "What can I do for you?"

Amy explained about Feather. "Can you check him out for us?"

"No problem," Scott replied. "I'll stop by tomorrow morning about ten. And how's the new rescue doing, that paint pony — Jigsaw?"

Amy thought about black-and-white Jigsaw. He had been a riding school pony until he'd developed a stress fracture in one of his front legs from overwork. Unable to work any more, he'd been sent to a sale. He'd been about to go for meat when an ex-client from the riding school had spotted him and had taken pity on him. She bought him and then contacted Heartland to ask if they would take him on. Amy and Ty had immediately agreed. "He's doing OK," Amy told Scott. "We've got him on cod-liver oil and alfalfa cubes to help increase his calcium intake, as well as thirty leaves and one cleaned root of white comfrey a day. Comfrey's great for treating bone damage."

"Yes, I remember your mom using it once on a horse with a stress fracture of the pelvis," Scott said. "A bay hunter."

"Arctic," Amy said, remembering. She never forgot any horse who'd been to Heartland. "He healed in three months."

"Let's hope Jigsaw's as lucky," Scott said. "I'll stop by his stall when I'm visiting tomorrow."

As Amy put the phone down, she found herself thinking how lucky they were to have Scott. Many vets ridiculed the type of treatments they used at Heartland, but Scott had always been interested in them. His attitude was, if it works then why not do it? Amy only wished that more people in the horse-world could be as open-minded.

"Where's Grandpa?" she asked, going to help Lou set the table.

"Taking a shower," Lou said. "He said supper should be ready in about ten minutes."

"Good. I'm starving!" Amy said.

Ten minutes later, Jack Bartlett, the girls' grandfather, came into the kitchen. "Ready to eat, you two?" he said, rubbing his hands.

"Definitely," Amy said, jumping to her feet and carrying over three plates.

Jack ladled out the Irish stew. He was a fantastic cook. For as long as Amy could remember, he had looked after the house and seen to the family's meals. Most of the time, he left the horses to Amy and Ty, but when it was needed, he put into the use the various skills he had learned as a cattle farmer before he had retired.

They sat down at the table. Lou picked up her knife and fork and then suddenly put them down again. "I wasn't going to tell you this yet," she said, a smile breaking out on her face, "but I just can't keep it to myself. I've had a brilliant idea of a way to increase Heartland's revenue."

"Tell us more?" Amy said, looking at her with interest.

Lou grinned. "Not yet. I want to find out if it's really possible first. I've arranged a meeting in town on Monday to check some things out – I'll tell you after that."

"At least give us a clue, Lou," Grandpa said.

But Lou shook her head secretively. "You'll have to wait

till Monday. But believe me, it's a great idea — you'll love it."
Her eyes shone happily. "If it works out like I think, we'll be
able to tell Daddy about it at the weekend and see what he
thinks."

Amy glanced at Grandpa. She knew he had never forgiven
Daddy for abandoning them. His jaw tightened but he
seemed to control his feelings. "What time's your father
coming on Saturday, Lou?" he asked.

"About ten o'clock," Lou said. "I can't wait. Can you, Amy?"

Amy made herself smile. She knew how much this visit
meant to Lou and she wasn't going to let her own feelings
spoil it. "No, it'll be good," she managed.

"I think I might go out for the day," Grandpa said.

"Go out?" Amy echoed, looking at him in alarm. It was
going to be bad enough meeting Daddy, but to do it without
Grandpa there! How could he? She needed him for moral
support.

"It's for the best," Grandpa said quietly.

Lou looked at him for a moment but then she nodded as
if she realized how much of a concession he was already
making in letting Tim, their father, visit Heartland. "OK,"
she said. "I understand. And we both appreciate you letting
Daddy come here, don't we, Amy?"

No, we don't, Amy wanted to shout. *Why couldn't you just
have said no, Grandpa?* But she forced herself to smile. "Yeah —
thanks, Grandpa," she said, hoping her voice didn't sound as
high and false to Lou as it did to her.

* * *

When Amy went up to her bedroom that night, she took up an old photo album. In it were snapshots of the family before Tim's accident – the accident at the showjumping World Championships that had left him too badly injured ever to ride professionally again. It had been after his accident that he had abandoned his family. After facing up to the fact that he wasn't coming back, Marion reluctantly sold up in England and returned to her childhood home in Virginia with three-year-old Amy. Lou, eleven years old at the time, had begged to be allowed to stay on at her English boarding school, believing that one day Daddy would return for her.

Amy turned the pages of the album. One photo in particular caught her eye. It showed Lou and herself mounted on two ponies. Amy studied it. There she was, a skinny three-year-old with jodhpurs that were way too big for her, and there was eleven-year-old Lou, her blonde hair in two chunky plaits, grinning from ear to ear as she clutched a silver trophy.

Amy looked at the joy and happiness on her sister's face, it seemed almost unbelievable that the girl in the picture could have grown up into her serious, reserved sister. And she was riding a pony and looking so natural and at home on him. It was like looking at a different person.

Amy's eyes moved to her parents. Marion stood beside Amy's pony, an arm flung casually round its neck, fair hair blowing in the breeze, mouth and eyes laughing. A stab of grief shot through Amy, and as tears blurred her vision she quickly looked away from her mom to where her dad was standing. Tall and dark-haired, he was smiling at Lou with a look of utter pride in his eyes.

Amy swallowed. He looked so handsome, strong and happy in the photo. *He sure has changed*, she thought, remembering back to the day last November when she had caught a brief glimpse of a tired old man at her mom's grave.

She shook her head. What would it be like meeting him again? What would she say to him?

A knock on the bedroom door startled Amy out of her thoughts.

"It's just me," Lou said, opening the door. "I'm going to make myself a hot chocolate. Do you want one?" Before Amy could answer, she saw the photo album on Amy's knee. "You've got Mom's old photos out," she said, walking over.

Amy nodded.

Lou looked at the photographs.

"Do you remember that day?" Amy asked, pointing at the photograph of the two of them on ponies

Lou nodded. "I'd just won an open jumping class. I remember being so glad that Daddy had been watching. I was determined I was going to be a showjumper just like him when I grew up."

"You look so happy," Amy said.

Lou nodded slowly. "I do, don't I?" she said at last. She shook her head. "Things used to be pretty simple back then," she said quietly.

Hearing a strange note in her sister's voice, Amy glanced at her. There was a look in her eyes that was hard to define — was it sadness, pain, loss? But before Amy had a chance to work it out, Lou had straightened up, the expression erased from her face.

"So, do you want a hot chocolate?" she asked abruptly.

"Uh … no thanks," Amy replied, taken aback by the sudden change in her.

"OK. Night then," Lou said briskly. "See you in the morning."

Amy watched her sister leave the room.

As the door shut she found herself wondering what exactly she had seen in Lou's eyes? It had been more than just sadness. Had there also been a look of — she searched for the right word — *regret*?

Chapter Three

At ten o'clock the next morning, Scott Trewin's blue jeep came bouncing up the driveway.

"Thanks for coming," Amy said, when he'd parked and got out. There weren't many vets that would call in for a routine visit on a Sunday, but Scott was amazing – he never seemed to mind the hours he spent with horses.

"No problem," he said, smiling warmly. "I'm on call anyway. So, where's this new pony you want me to look over?"

"In the barn," Amy said.

Just then, the back door opened and Lou came out. "Hey, there!" she said, coming over with a smile. "Amy said you were coming."

They kissed and then Scott grinned at Amy. "See, maybe I do have another reason for dropping by!" He looked at Lou. "Are you coming up to the barn with us?"

Lou nodded and they started to walk up the yard. Scott caught sight of Rosie, resting her head over her stall door. "Another new one?" he said.

"Yeah." Amy told him about Rosie's headshyness. "She just won't let you put anything near her ears. She's got a scar on one of them so I'm guessing she's had a bad experience in the past."

"Do you want me to look her over while I'm here?" Scott volunteered.

"Don't worry," Amy said, not wanting to use up any more of Scott's precious free time. "Her owner got her checked out by her vet before she contacted us. He didn't find anything wrong with her, though he had to sedate her to get close."

They passed Ben, who was sweeping the feed-room. He called out a greeting to Scott but didn't stop working. It was Ty's day off and, as usual when someone had a day off, that meant there was a rush to get everything done.

Feather was looking over his stall door, his ears pricked, his eyes flickering from side to side.

"It's OK, fella. Easy now," Scott said, taking Feather's halter off the hook outside his stall and walking in.

Amy held Feather while Scott began to examine him. After listening to Feather's heart and lungs and checking his teeth, he began to feel carefully over the grey pony's body, starting at the top of his neck and working down methodically over his withers, back and loins.

"Well, there's no obvious soreness," Scott said to Amy and Lou, after running his hands down Feather's legs and over his head. "But let's take him out so I can see him move."

Amy led Feather out of the barn and trotted him up and down on the concrete so that Scott could check out the pony for any lameness. Feather had the beautiful action typical of an Arabian and he practically floated across the ground. Amy could certainly believe that he'd won ribbons in conformation classes.

"Well, he looks sound," Scott said. "Just hold him still for me on that piece of level ground, Amy."

Amy did as she asked, and Scott examined the pony from all angles, searching for any signs of unevenness in his body that could have suggested that Feather had a physical problem. But at the end of the examination, Scott shook his head and patted the pony. "Perfect – or as near as can be," he said. "I'll take a blood sample and test it just to be sure that there's no underlying problem, but he looks to be in great health."

Feather lifted his muzzle to Scott's face and snorted softly.

Amy smiled. Feather really was cute – she could see why Jo adored him so. "If you're not hurting somewhere, I guess we'd better start looking for another reason why you're misbehaving," she said to the grey pony. "Let's work out what else is going on in your mind."

"He seems quite highly strung," Scott commented. "Maybe something's scaring him – making him play up."

Amy nodded. Her mom had told her over and over again that the vast majority of behavioural problems were caused by horses either being in pain or being scared. "Ty thought that he looked the sort of horse to panic," she said. She looked at Feather. "I'll probably get a better idea what's going on in his head when I ride him."

Lou, who had watched the whole examination, frowned. "But what if he rears?"

Amy shrugged. "Better with me than with Jo." And clicking her tongue, she led Feather back to the barn.

Scott followed her, stopping to have a quick look at Jigsaw. The black-and-white pony was resting quietly in his stall, holding his left foreleg out in front of him with the weight being held on the toe.

"Poor thing," Scott said, as he looked at the injured pony. "He works his heart out at a riding school for six years, then this happens and they send him to a horse sale to go for meat."

Amy nodded. "It's not much of a life, is it?" she said. "Being a riding-school pony."

"Depends on the school, I guess," Scott said. "If a pony ends up at the sort of place that Jigsaw was at — where the ponies are worked until they break — then no, it can't be a good life."

"But they're not all like that," Lou put in quickly. "Some are excellent. The horses and ponies are well fed and cared for and work only a reasonable amount..."

She was interrupted by a high-pitched bleeping noise. Scott pulled a pager from his pocket and looked at the message that flashed across it. "Looks like I've got to go," he said. "There's a mare foaling over at Crow's Landing." He kissed Lou quickly. "I'll call you later," he said, then picked up his bag from outside Feather's stall and set off down the aisle at a jog.

Lou watched him go and then went over to Sugarfoot's stall. "So, what have you got planned for this morning?" she asked Amy, as she reached over the door and scratched the Shetland affectionately on the neck. Sugarfoot was the only pony that Lou ever showed any real interest in. He had been half-starved when he came to Heartland and Lou had helped nurse him back to health. Amy knew that since then he had held a special place in Lou's heart.

"First I think I'll work Rosie — see if I can start getting her over her headshyness," Amy said, answering Lou's question. She remembered their conversation the day before about Lou learning to treat the horses. "You could help me, if you want."

Lou shook her head and started to gabble. "I can't. I've got so much stuff to do — things to get ready for this meeting on Monday, invoices to sort out and I'm in the middle of setting up a new spreadsheet on the computer and—"

"It's OK, I get the picture," Amy interrupted, thinking that she should have known better than to even bother asking. She started towards the tack-room.

"Amy! Hang on!"

Amy stopped, wondering what Lou wanted.

"Maybe I have got time," Lou said, a faint flush of pink colouring her pale cheeks as she left Sugarfoot's stall. "Just for a little bit." Amy stared at her in astonishment. "What ... er ... would you like me to do?"

"Well, I was going to groom Rosie first," Amy said. "You could give me a hand with that."

"OK."

Rosie was standing at the back of her stall when they arrived there with the grooming bucket.

"Good girl," Amy said, clipping a lead-rope on to Rosie's halter ring and tying her up.

Lou picked up a rubber curry-comb and, after a moment's hesitation, swept it over the filly's flecked neck and shoulder. "So, how are you going to help her?" she asked.

"Well, I'm fairly sure that she's acting up because she's frightened," Amy said, picking up a brush and starting to tease out Rosie's sparse chestnut tail gently. "There's a scar on one of her ears, so I think something happened to her in the past that scared her. What we have to do first is win her trust."

"By joining-up with her?" Lou asked, her curry strokes gradually becoming more confident.

Amy nodded. Joining-up was a technique that her mom had used a lot. It involved communicating with horses using body language. "Once I've got her trust, then I can start working on handling her ears and putting a halter on and off."

"She seems really quiet," Lou commented as she began to work on Rosie's hindquarters. "You wouldn't guess she was only three."

"I know," Amy said. Rosie had rested her muzzle on a ledge that ran round the stall wall. Like the day before, her eyes were half-closed. Amy felt a flicker of concern. Lou was right, the filly was really very quiet. There wasn't something wrong with her, was there? No, she told herself. Sheri's vet would have spotted it — after all, he'd only checked her out a day or so ago.

"She is OK, isn't she?" Lou said, standing back and frowning at the filly.

"Yeah, I'm sure she is," Amy replied. "Appaloosas were bred to be sensible and obedient."

Still, just to be sure, she took Rosie's temperature when they finished grooming. But it was normal. She shrugged and led Rosie up to the circular ring.

Once in the ring, she unclipped the long-line from Rosie's halter and, coiling it neatly, she clicked her tongue and waved it at Rosie's flank. The filly looked at her in mild surprise but, apart from shifting her hindquarters ninety degrees, didn't move.

"Go on!" Amy said, raising her arms and stepping towards her.

With a slight toss of her head, Rosie turned and trotted away.

Amy walked after her and swung the coiled rope in the direction of Rosie's hindquarters again.

Rosie began to trot round the ring. She tossed her head, several times. Keeping her shoulders square-on to the filly and her eyes on the filly's face, Amy urged her on. With another shake of her head, Rosie broke into a canter. Every time she tried to slow down, Amy stepped towards her, swinging the coiled long-line. The aim of joining-up with a horse was to get it to choose to be with the human in the middle, instead of running away by itself. Only then could she use her body language to show the horse that she was not a threat, and give the horse the chance to ask to be friends.

After four circuits, Amy moved so that her body was ahead of Rosie's and, raising her arms, she sent the filly round in the other direction.

After another five circuits, Amy got the signal she had been waiting for. The Appaloosa's inside ear flopped down, pointing towards her. She cantered round, her ear seeming to be fixed on Amy. After three more circuits, she began to lower her head. She was trying in her own language to tell Amy that she didn't want to run away from her any more. Finally her mouth opened and, slowing to a trot, she started to chew on the air. It was the signal Amy had been waiting for.

Dropping her arms, she immediately turned her body sideways on to the horse and lowered her eyes to the ground. *I am not a threat*, her body language was saying to Rosie. *If you want me to be your friend, then I will be.*

She heard the thud of the Appaloosa's hooves slow down from a trot to a walk and from a walk to a halt. Although she was behind Amy, Amy could sense that she was looking at her. She waited. One second passed, and then two and then three, and then she heard a soft snort and the sound of the filly's hooves on the sand.

Amy held her breath. And then she felt what she'd been waiting for — a gentle nuzzling at her shoulder.

Very slowly she turned and, still keeping her eyes averted, she rubbed the filly's nose.

"Good girl," she whispered. Then she turned and walked across the ring. Rosie walked after her, her nose nudging against Amy's shoulder. Wherever Amy went, Rosie followed. There was no rope keeping her at Amy's side — she was there because she chose to be. Amy swallowed the happiness bubbling up inside her. Nothing could ever compare to this moment, the moment when a horse overcame its instinct to run away, and volunteered its friendship. It was the beginning of a partnership based on trust.

She stopped and stroked Rosie's neck. The filly nuzzled her hand, looking at Amy in wonderment. Amy had often seen that expression on the faces of horses she had joined-up with. The relief in their eyes, as if they were saying, *At last I've found a human who understands.*

"And I do," Amy whispered to the mare. "Or at least I'll do my best to try to."

"Wow!" Lou said from the gate, as Amy walked over with

Rosie following. "That doesn't get any less amazing the more times you see it."

Amy's eyes glowed. "You should try doing it." Suddenly she stared at Lou. "Why don't you? You could have a go with Rosie now."

Lou took a quick step back. "No," she said quickly. "I ... I wouldn't want to mess things up."

"But you wouldn't," Amy said, longing for Lou to experience the thrill of joining-up. "Come on – I'll show you what to do."

But Lou continued to shake her head. "No. I ... I'd rather not." She quickly changed the subject. "So, what are you going to do with Rosie now?" she asked. "I mean, will she let you touch her ears now that you've joined-up with her?"

"Probably not," Amy said, moving one hand experimentally towards the Appaloosa's ears. As she expected, the filly jerked her head away.

"Oh," Lou said, looking disappointed.

"Joining-up isn't a miracle cure for all problems," Amy explained. "It's best to see it as a step in the right direction. By joining-up with her I'll have made it easier to help her overcome her fear, because she knows I'm basically not a threat, but it's too deep-seated a fear to be overcome just by joining-up."

"So what do you do now?" Lou asked, looking fascinated.

"Now I give her a choice. She can accept my touch or she can move away from me, but if she moves away she has to stay away."

"I don't get it," Lou said.

"Watch," Amy said, leading Rosie back into the centre of the school. Once again she put her hand up by Rosie's ear. The second the filly shied away, Amy immediately raised her arms in the air and sent her cantering back round the pen. After three circuits, Rosie was giving the signals that she wanted to be allowed into the centre again. As her mouth started to open and close, Amy turned her shoulders inwards and, through her body language, invited the filly to approach.

Once Rosie had followed her round the ring a few times, Amy started to feel all over her body. Once again as Amy's hands reached her ears. Rosie shied back and once again, Amy raised her arms and sent her cantering round the outside.

"Do you see?" she called to Lou. "I'm giving her a choice. She can either choose to stay beside me and have her ears handled or she can choose to go away – it's up to her. But if she chooses to go away then she has to stay away until I'm ready to let her come in and be near me again. I'm not forcing her to have her ears touched, I'm letting her make the choice."

Three times, Rosie came in and then shied away when Amy tried to handle her ears. But on the fourth time of trying, she actually stood still and let Amy stroke the base of her ears.

"Good girl," Amy praised, rewarding the filly's good behaviour by immediately moving her hand away. She rubbed Rosie's neck and then tried again. Rosie stiffened but she stood still as Amy stroked around both ears.

"Wow!" Lou said. "That's a huge improvement."

"And it's all done without force," Amy said in delight. She patted Rosie's neck. "OK, girl. That'll do for today."

"So how long do you think it will take to cure her completely?" Lou asked as they led Rosie back down to her stall.

"Hopefully not that long," Amy said. "She might be OK in a week or so, though it always depends on the horse."

"Are you going to try and cure her head-tossing as well?" Lou said as Rosie lifted her muzzle and circled it swiftly through the air. "I noticed she was doing it a lot out in the ring."

Amy frowned. She'd been so focused on the joining-up that she hadn't really noticed Rosie shaking her head, but now Lou mentioned it, she realized the filly had been doing it quite a bit.

"She's not going to make much of a pleasure horse if she does it when she's being ridden," Lou commented,

Amy nodded. "You're right. I'd better give Sheri a ring and talk to her about it. See if she's noticed."

As Lou helped her to give Rosie a quick brush to remove the traces of sweat and dust, Amy felt a glow of contentment. *If only things could always be like this*, she thought as she watched her sister sweeping a body brush over Rosie's spotted flanks. It felt good sharing her thoughts on Rosie with Lou. So often it seemed as if they didn't have that much in common. Lou was always busy in the office while Amy was out on the yard. They hardly ever just chatted or hung out together. And for once, Amy noticed, looking at her sister's face, Lou actually looked relaxed.

After Rosie had been finished, Lou helped Amy groom two of the other boarders – Maddison, a show horse who hated being trailered, and Sovereign, a young Morgan who had come to Heartland to have his fear of traffic cured.

"You know," Lou said, as they finished off Maddison. "I've been thinking – I really enjoyed watching you with Rosie today. Perhaps I should get more involved with treating the horses."

Amy was surprised but pleased. "That would be great," she said.

Lou's eyes shone with a sudden enthusiasm. "It would, wouldn't it? I could specialize in some sort of treatment – one that you and Ty don't use that much, homeopathy or something like that. Or there's this form of treatment using magnets that I read about in a magazine. Maybe I could become Heartland's magnotherapy expert."

Amy felt a prickling of unease. She'd been imagining Lou helping her and Ty. She wasn't sure she wanted her sister to become an expert.

"What do you think?" Lou demanded.

Amy hesitated. "Well, perhaps," she said doubtfully. "But what about learning the treatments we already use first? You could help me and Ty – like Ben's doing." She saw Lou's face fall.

"You don't think it's a good idea, then," Lou said flatly.

"It's just a bit sudden," Amy said, trying to be tactful. "Maybe you could specialize in a few years' time — once you've got more experience."

A shutter seemed to fall over Lou's face. "It was a dumb idea," she said.

"It wasn't," Amy protested. "I'd like you to help more."

But Lou didn't seem to be listening. She put down the brush she was holding. "I'd better go in," she said. "I've got loads to do." She forced a smile. "What was I was thinking of? I'm busy enough as it is without taking on more responsibilities."

"So, you're not going to start learning about treating the horses?" Amy asked, as Lou headed for the stall door.

"I think it's best if I leave that to you and Ty," Lou said. And looking suddenly sad, she turned and walked away.

Amy watched her go. She felt bad. She'd have liked Lou to help more, just not to take over. But that was her sister's nature. Lou couldn't ever get just a little bit involved in anything — if she decided something was worth doing then she put every ounce of herself into it.

Amy sighed and carried the grooming box round to Jake's stall. She had just started grooming him when Jo came up the driveway.

"Hi," she said, jogging over. "I've come to see Feather. How is he? Have you done anything with him? Is he OK?" The words tumbled out in her eagerness. Before Amy could answer, Jo noticed Jake. "Wow!" she gasped, looking at the enormous Clydesdale. "He's big! What's he called?"

"Jake," Amy replied, trying to work out which order to answer the questions in. "Feather's OK. The vet checked him over earlier and said he seems just fine, but I haven't started work with him yet."

"So, where is he?" Jo asked, looking round eagerly.

"In the back barn," Amy said, throwing her grooming brush into a bucket. "Come on, I'll show you."

"I would just love to live in a place like this," Jo said, as they walked up the yard. "You are so totally lucky."

Amy smiled. "I know. So, how's your mom?"

"A nightmare," Jo said, rolling her eyes. "The way she keeps going on you'd think Feather was about to win the Most Dangerous Horse of the Year award."

"You did well to stay on him when he reared like that," Amy said. "How long have you been riding?"

"Since I was seven," Jo replied. "I wanted to start before that but Mom wouldn't let me. She wasn't even that keen on me starting then, but Dad persuaded her."

"So why doesn't your mom like horses?" Amy asked.

"She's scared of them," Jo sighed. "When she was four, my gran had a riding accident. She ended up in a wheelchair and the horse she was riding had to be put down. Mom's been terrified of horses ever since. I think if she had her way I'd have a hobby like –" she wrinkled her nose in disgust – "embroidery or stamp-collecting. She's been even worse about me riding since she and Dad split up last year. She just seems to want to protect me all the time." For a moment her face looked downcast. "I don't like Mom getting upset, but I can't not ride. I love horses and I love Feather most of all." They had entered the back barn. Suddenly Jo saw Feather's grey head looking over his door. "Feather!" she squeaked.

The pretty grey pony pricked his ears and whinnied. Jo raced down the aisle and flung her arms round his neck. "Hey, boy. How are you?" she said, kissing him several times on his soft nose. He nuzzled her.

"I think he's pleased to see you," Amy said.

"Not as much as I am to see him," Jo said. She hugged him hard. "He's my best friend and I don't care what Mom says, I'm never ever going to let him go."

Amy felt a chill of apprehension run through her at Jo's words. She hoped that she was going to be able to cure Feather. But what if she couldn't? What would Jo do then?

Chapter Four

"So how was Feather when you rode him?" Soraya Martin asked, as she sorted out Amy's books at their lockers the next morning. For most of the bus journey to Jefferson High, Amy had been so busy finishing her homework assignments that she hadn't had time to talk. It was only now that she'd finally started to fill her best friend in on the events of the weekend.

"Great," she replied, thinking back to her ride on Feather the day before.

"He didn't try to rear?" Soraya said, fixing her black shoulder-length curls off her face with a hair-clip.

"Not a hint," Amy said. Feather had obviously been well schooled and was very responsive. In fact, far from being a problem, he'd been a joy to ride.

Soraya looked puzzled. "So why was he so bad on Saturday, then?"

"I don't know," Amy admitted. "It's a bit weird. Jo watched me ride him yesterday and said that's how he normally is. He's apparently only reared a couple of times. But unfortunately her mom was watching each time, so now Mrs Newhart's convinced he's too dangerous to ride." She shut her locker and leaned back against it, frowning. "There's got to be something that's triggering his bad behaviour, but until he starts playing up, I'm not going to be able to find out what it is."

"Sounds like you're just going to have to wait," Soraya said.

Amy nodded. "The trouble is, Mrs Newhart said she's only going to give me until the end of the month. If he's not better by then she's going to make Jo sell him."

"Poor Jo," Soraya said, as they started along the busy corridor towards their classroom.

"I just hope we can cure him in time," Amy said.

"I'm sure you will," Soraya said reassuringly.

"Give me a break. Heartland? Cure a horse?" a familiar voice drawled from behind them. "That would be a first."

Amy swung round. Ashley Grant was standing by the lockers, her arms crossed, her perfectly groomed eyebrows raised in a disbelieving line. Beside her, stood her two friends, Jade and Brittany. They were grinning.

"Come on, Amy," Soraya said. "She isn't worth it."

But Amy ignored her. "We've helped more horses at Heartland than you ever will at Green Briar," she snapped, glaring at Ashley.

Green Briar was the hunter barn that was run by Ashley's mom and dad. Using strong discipline and force, her mom, Val Grant, specialized in producing push-button horses and ponies that could be relied upon to rack up the ribbons – she also had a side-line in dealing with horses with behavioural problems. However, her methods were very different from those used at Heartland.

Ashley tossed her platinum-blonde hair over her shoulder and tutted. "Exaggerating again, Amy. Maths never has been your strong point, has it? We have three twenty-stall barns, four schooling rings, one covered arena and a cross-country course. And what do you have at Heartland? Let me see," she pretended to think. "Well, there's a single barn, a falling-down stable-block and two scrappy little rings. Yeah, I think we might just have dealt with a few more horses than you."

Despite the blood that was beating through her brain, Amy stared at her coolly. "I didn't say *dealt with*, Ashley, I said *helped*. You and your family don't know the meaning of the word." She saw Ashley stiffen slightly as her words hit home, and turned to go.

"Meaning you do?" Ashley said, recovering herself quickly. "Oh yeah, Amy, I'm sorry, I forgot. You're a horse-whisperer, aren't you?"

Jade and Brittany giggled.

Amy glared at her. She didn't like it assumed that she just whispered to horses and then they did what she said. She didn't do anything of the sort – she listened to what horses tried to communicate to her. "I am not a horse-whisperer," she said hotly. "I don't— Ouch!" She exclaimed as Soraya elbowed her in the ribs. Amy turned on her friend. "What are you...?"

But before she could finish, she realized why Soraya had nudged her. Matt Trewin — one of their best friends and, much to Amy's disgust, Ashley's current boyfriend — was approaching. "What's happening?" he enquired, a frown on his easy-going face as he looked from Amy to Ashley.

"Nothing," Amy said quickly. When Matt had first started dating Ashley, she had almost lost his friendship by telling him what she thought of his choice of girlfriend. Since then, she'd been trying to hold in her dislike of Ashley — at least when Matt was around.

The snideness vanished from Ashley's face. "We were just talking," Ashley said, going over and taking Matt's arm possessively. "In fact, I was just about to tell Amy some good news."

Amy caught a smug look in Ashley's eyes that suggested that whatever the news was, Amy certainly wasn't going to class it as "good". "What?" she said suspiciously.

"Oh, just that we might be seeing much more of each other in the future," Ashley said. "Daddy's heard there's some land coming up for sale just beside Heartland and he's going to put in an offer. He thinks it would be perfect for us to extend our facilities. He wants to build a combined-training centre."

"What?" Amy stared at her. "Which land?"

"The Youngs' farm," Ashley told her.

"I didn't know that was for sale!" Amy exclaimed, thinking of the fields to the east of Heartland.

"Well, why would they tell you?" Ashley said. "I mean, it's not like Heartland could afford to buy it, is it?" Her green eyes danced at Amy, as if daring her to have an outburst in front of Matt. "Won't it be nice?" she cooed, in a voice that dripped with saccharine-sweetness. "We'll be neighbours, Amy."

Amy saw Matt glance swiftly at Ashley. He wasn't stupid and, although she knew he desperately wanted to believe that she and Ashley had called a truce, she was sure that he knew exactly how things were between them.

"Lost your voice, Amy?" Ashley said, the triumphant taunt in her voice only barely concealed.

Amy bit back the sharp words that sprang to her tongue. She wasn't going to be goaded into a fight in front of Matt. "No, Ashley," she said coolly. "It's just that I like to think before I speak — something you rarely do."

And with that, she took hold of Soraya's arm and walked away.

"Wow!" Soraya said, as soon as they had turned the corner. "I thought you were going to freak when she talked about that farm, but you were awesome. You kept so cool!"

Amy stopped at the water-cooler and took a deep breath. "But do you think she could be telling the truth? Do you think the Youngs could be selling their land?"

"I don't know," Soraya looked doubtful. "You know what Ashley's like – full of a lot of hot air most of the time. I'm sure you would have heard about it if there was anything in it."

"You're right," Amy said. "Ashley's probably just trying to wind me up. I won't think anything more of it. Now, come on, we've got a maths class to get to!"

Ty was grooming Dancer when Amy got back from school that afternoon.

"Hey there," he called. His tousled hair had fallen over his forehead, and as Amy went over to him she had to fight a sudden urge to straighten it.

"So how was school?" Ty asked her.

"Same as always." Amy suddenly remembered her news. "Though you'll never guess what Ashley told me…"

She relayed what Ashley had said.

"Green Briar next door!" Ty said. "No way! Anyway, I'm sure we'd have heard about it if the Youngs really were selling their farm."

"I know," Amy agreed. "That's what Soraya said. Even so, it's too deeply scary to even think about." She shuddered. "Tell me something good. How have the horses been today?"

"All fine," Ty replied. And he started giving her a run-down on what he and Ben had been doing. "I haven't done anything with Rosie and Feather," he finished. "I thought it best to wait till you got home."

Amy nodded. "I'll work them in the school," she said. "Then maybe we could take Moochie and Sundance out for a ride?"

"Sure," Ty agreed with a smile.

An hour and a half later, Amy and Ty rode out of Heartland.

"We had a phonecall this morning from a woman asking if we had any horses that needed rehoming," Ty said, as they headed on to the trail that led up Teak's Hill, the wooded mountain behind Heartland. "She wants a horse for pleasure riding." He patted Moochie's neck. "I thought Moochie might suit her. She wants to know when she can come and visit."

"Tell her she can come and see him at the —" Amy broke off. She'd been about to say on the weekend, but suddenly she remembered about her father's visit. "A week on Sunday," she corrected herself and she fell into silence, her fingers playing in Sundance's dark mane

She'd been so busy all day that she'd almost forgotten about her father's visit, but there was no getting round the fact. Every second that passed was bringing the weekend closer.

"Thinking about your dad?" Ty asked, riding Moochie up alongside her.

Amy looked at Sundance's golden ears. "Why does he have to come? We're happy without him. Mom never wanted him here. When he wrote to her, she didn't reply. She didn't want him back in our lives."

"I know," Ty said. "But Lou does."

Amy nodded slowly. He was right. She was doing this for Lou. That's what she had to remember.

As they got back from their ride, Lou was just getting out of her car. She'd been at her meeting in town and, judging from the excited expression on her face, Amy guessed that it had gone well.

"So, are you going to tell me about it now?" she asked Lou.

"You bet I am," Lou grinned. "Amy Fleming – we might just be about to buy ourselves some more land. The Youngs are selling their farm. Come on, I'll tell you all about it over supper!"

Chapter Five

"A riding school!" Amy exclaimed. She stared at her sister in utter astonishment and growing horror. "Your plan is to have a riding school, Lou?"

Lou nodded, her eyes glowing enthusiastically as she looked from Grandpa to Amy. "Yeah, isn't it a brilliant idea? I can't believe Mom never thought of it. It will bring in money to help pay for the rehabilitation side of things, and we can even use some of the horses and ponies we rescue. It was when Jigsaw came that I had the idea," she said. "It would be so easy. We could get more ponies like him, make them better and then use them to give riding lessons on."

Amy shook her head. "It won't work. The horses we rescue are either traumatized or physically damaged. A pony like Jigsaw's never going to be fit for anything but light work."

Lou's face fell for a moment but then it brightened again.

"Well, we could look for horses and ponies who aren't as badly injured as Jigsaw," she said. "There are lots of sales on. We could find horses that just need some feeding up and conditioning. Anyway, that's why I had this meeting today. I heard the Youngs were selling some of the land that adjoins Heartland, so I arranged a meeting with the bank and they've agreed to give us a loan – well, in principle, anyway. We'll have money to buy the land, find some horses, hire a trainer and another stable-hand. Of course, we'll need to use Heartland as collateral and prepare a proper business plan before the bank will formally agree, but—"

"You mean you went to the bank to secure a loan using Heartland, and you didn't even ask me?" Jack's words cut through the air.

Lou stared at him, colour creeping up into her cheeks. "I didn't think you'd mind. You've always said that you'd leave the business side of Heartland up to me, Grandpa."

"I didn't mean deciding something like this!" Jack exclaimed. "Whether we should have a brochure and what sort of fund-raising event we should have is one thing, but raising a loan on the farm is quite another. Heartland belongs to me. It's my land."

Lou bit her lower lip and looked down at her plate. "I'm sorry, Grandpa. I ... I just wanted to see if it was possible. I was only trying to do what I thought was best."

Grandpa's voice softened. "I know you did, honey," he said covering her hand with his own. "And I'm not saying no to your idea. I'm just saying that we need to talk about it before we go steaming ahead."

"We sure do!" Amy exclaimed, suddenly recovering from the shock she was feeling and realizing she had to speak out. "I don't want a riding school here."

"Why not?"

The surprise in Lou's eyes seemed genuine and although Amy felt like shouting at her, she forced herself to keep calm. "It will get in the way of the work we do."

"But it doesn't have to," Lou protested. "In fact, it could complement it. You could teach the riding-school students about alternative therapies and they could help out on the main yard in the vacations and at weekends."

For a moment, Amy considered it. Maybe they could have a riding school where the ponies were happy and the students learned to listen to horses. *Yes, but it would mean Heartland getting bigger*, another part of her argued, *we'll have to have more staff and there'll be people coming and going all the time. Do you really want Heartland to be like that?* "I ... I'm not sure, Lou," she said.

"Look," Lou said. "Let me at least do the business plan. It will take me most of the week, and that will give you both some more time to think about it. If we decide that we don't want go ahead then we just won't take it any further."

"OK," Jack said slowly. He glanced across at Amy. "Is that all right with you? We can think about it some more and then decide."

Amy nodded. "Look, there's something else you should know." She frowned. "We might not get this extra land anyway, Lou. Ashley Grant told me at school today that her dad wants to buy it to extend Green Briar."

Lou looked worried. "We'd better get a move on then," Lou said. "I might go and speak to the Youngs and let them know we're interested. Maybe we can come to some arrangement before it goes on the open market." Her eyes shone as she looked round at them. "I know this can work — I just know it!"

"Have you told Ty about Lou's plan?" Soraya asked the next day, as they had lunch in the cafeteria.

Amy nodded. "I rang him last night."

"What did he say?"

Amy moved closer so she could speak over the noise of the other students. "He wasn't pleased but he says that if it happens, it happens." She sighed. "I know Lou's good at business, but sometimes she just gets so hung up on bringing in money. She doesn't think about whether it's a good idea for other reasons."

Soraya nodded. "It must be tough for her. I guess she's still trying to prove herself."

"What do you mean?" Amy asked in surprise.

Soraya tucked a stray curl behind her left ear and looked thoughtful. "Well, she had that big job in New York before she came back to Heartland. I can see why she isn't content to just do the accounts and things. I guess she wants to make her mark – to be as successful at Heartland as she was in the city. Particularly seeing as your dad's coming. She's going to want him to feel proud of her, isn't she?"

Amy stared at her friend. "I hadn't thought about it like that before, but you could be right." She grimaced. "I just wish it didn't mean her coming up with ideas like this. I can't say no because I know it means such a lot to her, but I don't want to say yes."

"Well, maybe the Grants will get the land," Soraya said.

"Thanks a bunch," said Amy, getting up to dump her rubbish. "That's so not a solution!"

"So how are you feeling about your dad coming?" Soraya asked as they walked out into the school grounds.

"I don't want to think about it," Amy said, with a shudder. She changed the subject quickly. "Ben asked about you last night. Wanted to know where you'd been."

"Did you tell him I was rehearsing for this play?" Soraya said quickly. She had the lead in the forthcoming school play and hadn't been to Heartland as much as usual.

"No, I told him you were on the moon." Amy grinned. "What do you think I said?" She shook her head. "You know, I wish you two would just get it together."

"That would be fine by me," Soraya said. "Anyhow, you can talk. Look at you and Ty. I don't know why you don't just admit you like each other and start dating properly."

"I don't want to," Amy protested. "You know what people

are like when they date. I don't want to be forever talking and thinking about him, and worrying about our relationship."

At that moment, Soraya saw Matt, who was standing with Ashley by the school gates. She shot Amy a sideways look. "I wonder how Matt would take the news that you and Ty are dating. After all, didn't you tell him that wouldn't go out with him because you didn't want to risk your friendship?"

"Yeah," Amy said uncomfortably. "But Matt doesn't like me any more. He's got Ashley now."

"Like that's going to last!" Soraya said. "Did you hear her bossing him around this morning after biology? He's not going to stand for that sort of treatment for long."

Amy raised her eyebrows. "He seems to be coping pretty well right at this moment," she said, as Matt put his arm round Ashley's shoulders.

After school, Amy got changed and then worked Rosie in the ring. Although it was only three days since she had first joined-up with her, the filly was already much better at having her ears handled and a halter put on. As usual, Amy started the session with a join-up, and then, once Rosie was willingly following her around, she started to stroke the filly's head. Working her fingers in small circles, she reached Rosie's ears. Still, Rosie stood there. Trying hard to keep her breathing relaxed, Amy unbuckled the halter. Rosie started slightly as it slid off her nose.

"Easy now," Amy soothed.

She brought the halter up to the mare's nose again. But the movement was too much for Rosie. With a snort she shied away. "OK then, off you go," Amy said, raising her arms and sending the mare trotting round the ring. As she kept the mare going, she found herself wondering what Tim, her father, would say when he saw how they worked with the horses at Heartland. Her mom had only got into using alternative therapies through trying to help Pegasus, Tim's great showjumper. Conventional medicine had only helped him so much, and then Marion had begun to search for other solutions. It was the knowledge she had gained through treating Pegasus that led to Heartland helping other damaged horses.

Amy thought about her father. *He's probably into traditional training techniques*, she thought bitterly. *He won't understand our work at all*.

It only took a few circuits before Rosie started to let Amy know that she wanted to be allowed to come in close again. This time when Amy tried with the halter, the filly stood still and let her slip it on and buckle it up.

"Good girl," Amy praised in delight.

"She's really coming along," Ty's voice said behind her.

Amy turned. "Isn't she?"

"Still tossing her head though," Ty said, as Rosie circled her head in the air.

"I know," Amy said. She'd spoken to Sheri about it, but Sheri had said she'd never noticed it.

"Hi!" They turned to see Jo-Ann jumping out of her brother's car and coming up the yard.

"Hello," Amy called.

"Have you ridden Feather this morning?" When Amy shook her head, Jo said, "Could I groom him, then?"

"Sure," Amy replied.

Jo ran back down the yard and Ty smiled. "She's a nice kid."

"Yeah – really nice," Amy said. "And she's picking up on the T-Touch well. She's been doing it on him each night, and massaging in the violet-leaf oil like I showed her. He seems to love all the fuss."

"But we're still no further towards working out what the problem is," Ty said.

"No," Amy said. "Until he misbehaves there's not much that I can do," she said. "Maybe tonight will be the night."

But Feather was as good as ever. He walked, trotted and cantered in serpentines and figure of eights. Amy even popped him over a small jump, and there wasn't a hint of him playing up.

"It's like he can read my mind," Amy said, stopping by the fence to talk to Jo. "I only have to think about turning or changing pace and he does it." She patted his neck. "You're one cool pony, Feather." He snorted and nodded his head.

Jo laughed. "See, he understands every word you say." She looked at him longingly. "Can't I ride him?" she begged. "Mom would never know."

Amy reluctantly shook her head. "Sorry, but you know what your mom said. Not until we're really sure that he's safe."

"But it's so unfair!" Jo exclaimed. She caught Amy's look and piped down a little. "I just want to ride him so much," she sighed.

For the rest of the week, Feather continued to behave perfectly. By Friday, Amy was at her wits' end. "We've only got three weeks left with him, Ty, and we still don't know why he reared with Jo," she said, feeling frustrated as they filled the evening haynets. "And with my —" she almost muttered the word — "father here this weekend I probably won't have that much time to work him."

"Perhaps we should get Jo to ride him," Ty said. "See what he does."

Amy pulled the draw-string on the haynet tight. "OK, maybe I'll give Mrs Newhart a ring tonight and see what she says."

"Didn't Jo say she and her mom were out of town for the weekend?" Ty said.

"Oh yeah," Amy said, remembering that Jo had told her she wouldn't be down at the yard again till Monday. "I'll ring Monday, then."

Lou came into the feed-room. She had a notebook and pencil. "I've got a few questions to ask you," she said.

Amy groaned inwardly. Ever since Lou had started

preparing the business plan for the bank she'd been constantly asking questions about the riding school.

"Now, how many hours do you think a pony could work each day?" she said. "And how much feed would each pony need?"

The questions went on, until Amy wanted to scream. The more Lou talked about a riding school, the less she wanted one at Heartland.

But what can I say? she thought as she went into the house. Before she went inside, she took a last look round at the yard. Ty and Ben, obviously sensing her anxiety at meeting her father the next morning, had tidied the whole place up. Amy felt really touched by their efforts.

"It's not as if I care what he thinks," she muttered as she pulled off her boots.

Going into the house, she met Grandpa. He was just about to go out for dinner with Ken and Marie, some friends of his, and his usual jeans and sweater had been replaced by a duck-egg-blue open-necked shirt and chinos. "I'd better get moving," he said, picking up his car keys from the counter. "Lou's gone to Scott's for the evening. Are you sure you'll be OK on your own?"

"I'll be just fine." Amy said, flopping down in one of the armchairs. "You have a good time."

"Thanks. There's some ham in the refrigerator for supper." He came over and kissed the top of her head. "I'll see you later."

Jack went out through the door and a few minutes later, Amy heard him drive away.

The room seemed suddenly very quiet. She leaned her head against the back of the armchair. She hardly ever spent evenings on her own. What should she do?

Eat first, she decided, as her stomach growled loudly into the silence.

She got to her feet and made up a couple of bagels with some of the ham that Grandpa had baked and a carton of cream cheese. Putting them on to a plate, she went upstairs. Maybe she should get started on her weekend homework.

But when she sat down at the desk and opened her history book, the words she was reading just refused to go into her head. She kept thinking about the next day and meeting her father. After she had read and re-read the first paragraph five times, she finally gave up.

Closing her history book, she picked up a photograph of her mom that she kept on her desk. It showed her standing by Pegasus's pasture gate. The big grey thoroughbred was nuzzling her mom's fair hair, and Marion was laughing. It had been taken just a few weeks before the accident.

"Oh, Mom," Amy whispered, touching the picture with her lips. "What would you say if you knew Daddy was coming here tomorrow? What would you tell me to do?"

She shut her eyes. But there was no answer. She was on her own.

Chapter Six

"You're going to spend the weekend with Ken and Marie!" Amy exclaimed, staring at Grandpa the next morning.

Jack nodded. "You know they've just moved house, and it sounds like they could really use a hand getting their yard in order," he said. "I've offered to put in some runs up for their dogs. It'll be easier all round if I stay there overnight."

"But what about Daddy?" Lou said. "You won't see him at all if you're away all weekend."

"I know, but I've thought about it and I think it's for the best," Jack said. "You two need some space with your father on your own." Lou opened her mouth. "I've made up my mind, Lou," Jack said, before she could argue. "And I'm not going to change it."

Lou looked at his stubborn face. "All right," she said reluctantly. "If you're sure it's the right thing to do."

Grandpa nodded. "Believe me, it is."

As he left the kitchen to get his things together, Lou picked up a cloth from the sink and started to wipe over the kitchen table. "This place needs tidying up before Daddy gets here."

Amy grabbed her jacket off the back of the door and went outside. Maybe keeping busy would help keep her butterflies at bay too.

At quarter to ten, Amy left Ty and Ben to finish off the remaining stalls and reluctantly went inside to shower. When she came downstairs, Lou was hovering by the kitchen window. Every surface was spotless and on the table was a vase of freshly cut flowers.

Not knowing what to do with herself, Amy sat down at the table. It was impossible to sit still. Every nerve in her body felt stretched to breaking point. She bounced one foot up and down on the floor, and, when that didn't help, she started to drum her fingers on the table-top.

"Amy!" Lou snapped, swinging round. "Stop that!"

Amy looked up with a start.

Lou's face softened. "I'm sorry," she sighed. "I guess I'm just a bit tense."

"It's OK," Amy said. "Me too." She got to her feet and walked restlessly around the kitchen. The butterflies were getting worse now. She could feel a wave of panic swelling inside her.

I don't want to be here, she thought, *I don't want him to come here*.

But it was too late.

"Here he is!" Lou said, her voice rising in excitement as she flew to the door.

Amy followed, her heart pounding. A silver Lexus had just parked outside the house and a tall man was getting out.

"Daddy!" Lou gasped.

For a moment, Amy thought that Lou was going to run and fling her arms round his neck. But at the last minute something seemed to stop her. "Hello," she said, coming to a halt at the front of the car.

"Lou," Tim Fleming said, his English accent sounding clipped and precise. He walked towards Lou, and shook his head wonderingly. "How lovely to see you!" he said, taking her hands. "My, how you've grown." His eyes lifted and he looked at Amy. "Amy?"

Wishing she was somewhere — anywhere — else, Amy nodded. Her father came over to her, his gaze riveted on her face. He reached out for her hands too, but Amy kept them firmly in her pockets.

Tim's hands dropped, but his eyes continued searching her face. "I can't believe it's you," he said.

Maybe that's because you haven't seen me in twelve years, Amy thought, but she kept the sharp answer to herself. She shrugged. "Well, it is."

He had changed so much from the photos. His tanned

skin was carved into deep grooves and lines, and his grey eyes looked shadowed.

"Should we go inside and have a coffee?" Lou said, coming over.

Tim nodded. "That would be nice."

Amy followed them into the kitchen. While Lou set about making drinks, Tim looked at the photographs on the kitchen wall. "I remember that," he said, putting his finger on one of the framed photographs of Marion jumping at Hickstead – an international show in England.

Don't touch it! Amy wanted to snap.

"Your mother was a brilliant showjumper," Tim said, turning to her.

"I know," Amy said coldly. "Grandpa told me."

"Where is Jack?" Tim asked.

"He's gone away for the weekend," Lou said quickly. "He ... he had to help some friends out."

Tim sighed. "And he didn't want to see me."

Lou fumbled with the coffee-maker. "It wasn't like that," she began. "These friends of his, they've just moved house and—"

"It's OK, Lou," Tim interrupted. "You don't have to make excuses. I can understand Jack might not want to see me."

"Like you can blame him," Amy said, the words darting out of her before she could stop them.

"Amy!" Lou said.

Amy looked mutinously at the floor, but not before she had caught Tim glancing quickly in her direction.

There was an awkward silence for a moment and then Tim cleared his throat. "Well, Lou, do you want a hand with that coffee?"

"It's OK," Lou said. "It's nearly ready."

Amy could hear the irritation in Lou's voice and knew that it was because of her. Mentally, she kicked herself. She hadn't meant to make Lou mad. Why couldn't she just have kept her thoughts to herself? "I'll help you, Lou," she offered, keen to make up.

Lou's frosty expression thawed slightly. "Thanks."

They put out the cups and the milk, and Lou poured the coffee. "White with one sugar?" she said, smiling at Tim. "I remember how you like it."

"Actually, Lou," Tim said, putting his hand over the cup before she could add milk. "Just black would be fine."

"Oh, right," Lou said, looking slightly taken aback.

For a moment no one spoke, and then Lou broke the silence.

"You said on the phone at Christmas that your wife's just had a baby," she said to Tim. "Have … have you brought any photographs with you?"

"Yes, I have," Tim said, a sudden smile turning up the corners of his mouth. He pulled his wallet out of his pocket. "Here she is," he said, proudly, as he handed them a photo of a baby with a shock of light-brown hair. "She's called Lily."

"She's so sweet," Lou said quietly.

Tim looked at Amy. "She's just like you when you were that age."

Amy stared at the baby in the photograph. It was just too weird to think that she and the baby were half-sisters. She placed the photograph on the kitchen table without saying a word.

"And this is one of the two of you when you were little," Tim said, taking out another photograph and showing it to them. It was a picture of them playing on a beach together when Amy was about three. Amy had seen a similar one in her mom's photo album. "I carry it everywhere with me," Tim said quietly.

The silence seemed to swell as Amy and Lou looked down at the old photograph. Finally, Tim cleared his throat. "So ... er, Amy," he said, picking up the photographs and putting them away. "How are you doing at school?"

"Fine," Amy muttered, her thoughts whirling.

Tim waited as if expecting her to say more. When she didn't he just nodded. "Right, good." He cleared his throat again. "And, Lou. You said in your letter that you used to work in Manhattan."

"Yes. I was with Citibank," Lou said, seeming to come out of a trance. "I did an MBA when I finished at Oxford and then I got a job over here. I'd been working for Citibank for just over a year when –" she hesitated – "when Mom had her accident."

Tim nodded. "Then you gave it all up to come back here."

"That's right," Lou said. "I wasn't sure I'd done the best thing for a while. I loved the buzz of working in New York." As she spoke, her eyes glowed.

"I see," Tim said, but Amy thought his tone suggested he was agreeing more out of politeness than because he really understood how Lou felt.

"Anyway," Lou went on. "Now I run the business side of things here. I'm actually in the middle of developing a business plan to start a riding school – if we can get a loan sorted out to buy the land we need."

"We're not actually committed to it yet," Amy said quickly. She felt Tim glance at her but she kept her eyes on Lou. "Grandpa hasn't said yes."

"But he will," Lou said, shooting her a look that said quite clearly that Amy wasn't to argue. She smiled at Tim. "It's quite a big job, you know."

"It certainly is." Tim frowned slightly. "From what I've heard, I thought your main concern here was rescue horses."

"It is, but to run a sanctuary like this you need to bring in quite a bit of money," Lou said. "A riding school would be the perfect answer."

"I wouldn't have thought a riding school would bring in that much money," Tim said thoughtfully. "They're not known for being hugely profitable. Are you sure it's a wise decision?"

"Yes," Lou said sharply.

"Lou's right." Despite her doubts about the riding school,

Amy found herself leaping to her sister's defence, as she saw a look of hurt flickering through Lou's eyes. "Of course she's thought it all through. She wouldn't have suggested it otherwise."

Lou looked at her in surprise but then smiled gratefully.

Tim nodded uncomfortably, and didn't say anything more.

The silence stretched out. Unable to bear the tension in the room, Amy got to her feet. "Would you like to see the yard?" she offered.

Tim jumped to his feet. "That would be great."

As Amy led the way to the yard, she thought about this meeting with their dad. It wasn't really going like she'd imagined it at all. She'd thought that he and Lou would be talking non-stop about "the old days". But nothing could be further from the truth. There was only one word to describe the atmosphere, and that was awkward.

"So how many horses do you have here?" Tim asked her as they walked up to the front stable-block.

"Eighteen," Amy replied. "Eight rescue, eight boarders, my pony Sundance and Red over there," she nodded to the big chestnut who was looking out over his stall door. "He belongs to Ben — one of our stable-hands."

"Hello, boy," Tim said, going over and offering the back of his hand to the chestnut gelding. Red bent his head and snuffled at him. Tim rubbed his nose. "You're a fine-looking horse, aren't you?"

Although Amy didn't want to be over-friendly to her

dad, she couldn't help agreeing. "He is, isn't he? He's a Thoroughbred-Hanoverian cross. Ben competes him in High Prelim, but the way he jumps he's going to upgrade really quick."

Just then, Ben came out of the tack-room. Seeing that they were by Red's stall, he came over.

Lou introduced him to their father.

"Pleased to meet you, sir," Ben said, holding out his hand.

"Likewise," Tim said. "I was just admiring Red. He's certainly a looker. Amy says you jump him?"

"Yes," Ben said, his face lighting up at Tim's praise for Red. "I've had him since he was three. I backed him myself and I've been bringing him on since then."

"Good for you," Tim said, stroking Red's neck. "Maybe I could watch you ride him later on?"

"Sure!" Ben said, looking delighted. "I'll put some fences out at lunchtime."

Amy looked at Ben in surprise. Why was he looking so thrilled? Then it dawned on her. To Ben, her father was Tim Fleming, the former Olympic showjumper who had won all over the world. Of course Ben was delighted that he wanted to see Red jump.

Just then, Ty came down the yard to say hello.

"So how long have you been working here, Ty?" Tim said, as they shook hands.

"Three years," Ty replied.

"You must tell me about the work you do," Tim went on.

He looked at Amy. "You too, Amy. I've been getting into natural remedies over the last few years. I'd love a chance to pick your brains and learn some more."

Amy looked at her father suspiciously but he actually looked as if he meant what he'd said.

"Sure," Ty said. "I could talk about our techniques all day if you'd let me."

Tim smiled. "Sounds great." He looked around. "Do I get to meet the rest of the horses now?"

As Amy led the way round the rest of the yard, she felt herself relaxing slightly. Introducing her father to the horses was a hundred times better than sitting in the kitchen. For a start, he seemed to relax more around the horses and, she had to admit, he was very good with them. He didn't force his presence on them but waited until they came to say hello to him. Then, stroking them gently, he would murmur soft words to them. Without exception, they all responded.

Watching as even Rosie bent her head and allowed him to scratch her forehead, Amy felt surprised. For some reason, she hadn't expected him to be so good with horses. She should have known that he would be – after all, he had spent his life with them. But she'd grown up thinking of her dad as being everything that was opposite to her mom.

"Do you have any other stalls?" Tim said, as they walked out of the barn and over to the turn-out paddocks.

"No," Amy replied. She looked at him in surprise. There was something about his voice that suggested that he had been hoping that there would be some more.

"I see," Tim said. He was quiet for a moment, fussing over Maddison and Sovereign, who had come up to the gate to check for treats. "What ... er ... what happened to Pegasus?" he asked.

Amy suddenly realized that her father didn't know that Pegasus had died. And one thing her mom had always told her was that her dad had been devoted to his great show-jumping partner. Her mom's voice came back to her now. "I think that was one of the things that hurt Daddy the most after the accident. He couldn't bear the thought that he had hurt Pegasus so badly."

"Um..." she faltered, looking at Lou for support.

"He died in October," Lou said, coming over to join them. "We had to put him to sleep. He had cancer."

Amy looked at the back of her dad's head. For a long moment, he didn't speak.

"In October," he said at last. "So, I'm four months too late to see my boy."

Amy knew how he felt. Pegasus had been a horse in a lifetime. Once you loved him, you loved him for ever. She glanced round at Lou to see if she understood too, but her sister's lips had tightened.

"Yes, I'm afraid you are," she said briefly.

Tim didn't seem to notice the coolness in Lou's voice. "I'd hoped..." His voice trailed off. For a moment he stared out across the fields and then he gave a slight shake of his head and turned. "I've had an idea," he said. "Why don't we all go out for a ride together? It would be just like old times."

Amy's eyes flew to her sister's face.

"I ... I don't ride any more," Lou said quickly.

Tim frowned. "What do you mean you don't ride? Since when?"

Lou looked at the ground. "Since your accident."

"Since my accident?" Tim echoed. He stared at Lou. "Lou, this isn't really true, is it?"

Lou nodded.

"But you were on a horse before you could walk!" Tim exclaimed. A frown deepened the lines in his face. "Lou, are you scared because of what happened to me?"

"No!" Lou said looking up, her cheeks flaming.

"It was an accident, Lou," Tim said, his eyes scanning her face. "Nothing more. An accident that was my fault."

"I am not scared!" Lou exclaimed hotly.

Before Tim could say anything more, there was the sound of the phone ringing out on the yard. "I'll answer it," Lou said, sounding relieved.

"Leave it," Amy said. "Ben or Ty will get it."

But Lou was already hurrying down the yard.

"I think I've upset her," Tim said.

"She's just a bit weird about the riding thing," Amy said.

"Scared?" Tim asked.

"I ... I don't think so," Amy replied. "I mean, she's never said so."

Tim sighed. "I'd better go after her."

Amy followed him down to the kitchen. Lou was just putting the phone down. "A prospective client," she said, before Amy could ask. "Now," she said briskly, starting to tidy away the coffee cups as if nothing had happened. "We should start thinking what we want to eat. There's Grandpa's baked ham or a lasagne I cooked yesterday afternoon, which would—"

"Forget lunch, Lou," Tim interrupted her. "Look, I'm sorry if I upset you just now. It was just such a shock. You always used to loved riding so much."

"That was then," Lou said briefly. She saw Tim about to open his mouth again. "Please," she said, holding up her hand. "I'd really rather not talk about it. Now," she said, pulling the fridge door open, "what can I get you for lunch?"

Chapter Seven

Ty and Ben joined them for lunch, which lightened the atmosphere considerably. As Tim chatted about horses, Amy felt herself starting to warm to him just slightly. Perhaps the day wasn't going to turn out quite as badly as she'd imagined.

However, when the last coffee cup had been drained and Ty and Ben went back outside, a silence fell. Amy shifted in her chair, wishing she could leave the room.

"So," Tim said, rather awkwardly. "Here we are."

"Yes," Lou said. "Here we are."

Amy started counting the knots in the wooden table-top.

"Daddy," Lou said suddenly. "Can I ask you something?"

"Sure, fire away," Tim replied, leaning back in his chair.

Picking up a petal that had fallen from one of the flowers, Lou passed it from hand to hand. "Why did you never come and find me?" she asked at last. She looked up at him. "I mean, you knew where I was at school in England. Even if you didn't want to see Mom, why didn't you come and see me?"

"You stayed on at school in England?" Tim said, looking shocked.

"You didn't know?" Lou said slowly.

"No," Tim said. "I just assumed you'd moved to Virginia with your mother."

Lou shook her head. "I stayed on at my boarding school. I was sure you'd come and find me. I wanted to stay there because at least then you'd know where I was."

"I didn't realize," Tim said, staring at her. "I wrote to your mother about a year after she moved here. I wanted to know how you all were. She wrote back but she never told me that you were still in England."

"She didn't tell you?" Lou echoed, shock on her face. "But why?"

Tim shook his head. "I don't know. Maybe she didn't want to make it easy for me to have contact with you. Your mother had her weaknesses just like everyone else."

Amy stared. "No, she didn't!" she exclaimed. "And Mom would never have hurt Lou just to get back at you!"

A look of contrition fell instantly across Tim's face. "Amy..." he said, reaching for her hand

Amy jerked her hand away. "Don't you dare say anything against Mom!" she said, jumping angrily to her feet. "You were the one that left her!"

"I know, I know," Tim said. "I was just trying to help Lou to understand. I didn't mean to upset you. I'm sorry."

Amy felt like picking up the nearby vase of flowers and throwing it at him, but seeing Lou's shocked face, she fought the urge. She wouldn't ruin this day for Lou — she wouldn't. "Fine," she said, having to force the words out through clenched teeth.

"Can I get anyone a drink?" Lou said, in an obvious attempt to defuse the situation.

"Thank you. Just a glass of water," Tim said.

"Amy?"

Amy shook her head. She might have managed to stop herself losing her temper but right now she didn't want to spend another minute in her father's company. "I'm going to go help Ty and Ben," she said, making for the door.

Feeling almost too mad to speak, Amy marched up the yard. She stopped by the tack-room, but she knew she was in no state of mind to work a horse — or even to groom one. Instead she went into the feed-room and started to fill the haynets, stuffing great handfuls of hay into them with enormous force. *I hate him, I hate him, I hate him*, she repeated over and over again in her head, as she remembered his words.

"So what's up with you?" Amy turned and saw that Ty was watching her from the doorway.

"I don't want to talk about it," she said, almost spitting each word out.

"Is it your dad?" Ty said.

"What do you think?" Amy snapped.

Ty ignored her harsh words. "I thought you seemed to be getting on OK with him earlier," he said, coming over to her.

"Well, you're wrong!" Amy almost shouted. She saw Ty frown. "Look, I'm sorry," she said, raking her hands through her long hair. "I don't mean to take it out on you. It's just something he said. I think I need to be on my own for a bit." She managed a small smile. "Maybe I'll just beat up this hay some more."

Ty nodded understandingly. "OK," he said, squeezing her arm. "But if you need to talk," his green eyes searched hers, "you know I'm always here."

Warmth flooded through Amy's veins. "I know," she said gratefully.

Ty turned to go.

"Thanks, Ty," she called after him.

He threw a smile over his shoulder. "Any time."

After filling the haynets, Amy set to work on brushing the dried mud off the outdoor rugs. It was hard work and she was soon red in the face and dripping with sweat, but by the time all the rugs had been cleaned up, she was feeling much better. It didn't matter what her dad said. He was only here for the weekend, and then she need never see him again.

She was just hanging up the last rug when she heard footsteps outside the door.

"Amy?" Lou called.

Amy went out on to the yard. Lou and Tim were standing there.

"Dad's got to go in a few minutes," Lou said.

"But I'm going to come and visit again tomorrow," Tim said. "I'd love to see you ride then."

Amy nodded, but didn't speak.

"I meant to ask you at lunchtime," Tim said. "Do you compete in any shows?"

"Yes," Amy replied briefly. "I could have been going to one tomorrow." She only just stopped herself from adding that it would have been a million times better than spending the day with him.

Tim smiled. "I'm impressed. I wouldn't have missed a competition for anyone when I was younger – not for anything."

Amy didn't reply. The silence grew.

"Well – I'd better go," Tim said at last.

"Come and see Daddy off, Amy." Lou gave Amy a pleading look, and Amy reluctantly joined her sister at their father's side.

"Is it OK if I come round about ten again?" Tim asked as he opened the door of his rented car.

"Fine," Lou said.

For a moment, it looked like Tim was going to step forward and hug her, but then he seemed to change his mind. "See you tomorrow, then," he said, and he got into the car, shut the door and drove away.

"If I never see him again after this weekend it will be too soon!" Amy exclaimed, as his car disappeared out of sight. She turned to Lou. "Can't you go out for the day with him or something tomorrow? Or can't I go to the show? He doesn't need to see me again."

"Yes, he does," Lou said firmly. "You need to get to know each other."

"If he's going to say those sorts of things about Mom then I don't think I want to," Amy muttered.

Lou sighed. "Amy, I know today might not have been quite as perfect as we'd been imagining—"

"As you'd been imagining," Amy corrected her quickly. She frowned. "Anyway, why wasn't it perfect for you?"

Lou looked embarrassed. "I suppose it just wasn't quite like I'd thought it would be. But anyway, that doesn't matter," she said, her voice suddenly brisk. "It'll get better. I know it will. We just need some time to get to know each other again." She looked beseechingly at Amy. "Please, Amy — we've got to keep trying."

Amy looked at her for a long moment and then gave in. "OK, OK," she said. "I'll see him tomorrow if it makes you happy."

Amy was filling Jake's water-bucket at the tap near the house when Tim arrived the next morning. The back door opened. "You're early," Lou said, coming out. "It's only nine-thirty."

Tim smiled. "Well, I didn't see the point of staying in my

hotel when I could be here with you." He lifted a hand in Amy's direction. "Hey, there."

Amy felt like scowling but, knowing Lou was watching, she forced a smile on to her face. "Hi," she said coldly.

"Have you had breakfast? Can I get you anything to eat or drink?" Lou asked.

"No food," Tim said. "The hotel provided an enormous breakfast. But maybe a coffee?"

"Sure," Lou said. "Come in." She glanced across at Amy. "Are you coming too?"

Amy shook her head. "I can't. There's loads still to do." She saw Lou's eyes start to narrow. "Ben's at the show — I can't leave Ty to manage on his own," she said quickly, trying to ignore the guilty feeling that was sneaking up on her.

"If you're pushed, I can do without the coffee," Tim said suddenly. "Why don't I pitch in and give you a hand?"

It wasn't what Amy had been intending at all. She started to shake her head. "It's OK, don't worry—"

"It's not a problem," Tim interrupted, coming towards her. "Just tell me what to do." He smiled. "To tell you the truth I'd enjoy it. I hate being away from my yard when I'm on business." He glanced back at Lou. "You'll come and help too, won't you, Lou?"

Lou hesitated. "I guess so," she said at last.

"So what do you want me to do?" Tim asked Amy, as Lou went inside to change.

Amy swallowed. She hadn't really been telling the truth

when she'd said there was loads to do. Knowing that Ben would be away at the show, Ty had come into work early and most of the basic chores like mucking out and sweeping the yard had just about been done.

Tim misunderstood her silence. "I'm not proud. I don't mind mucking out or scrubbing buckets."

"Maybe you could groom a couple of horses for us," Amy faltered.

"Sure," he agreed easily. "Show me which ones."

Cringing inwardly, Amy led the way to the tack-room. She had a feeling that her father knew enough about the running of a yard to have now guessed that she had just been trying to use her supposed busyness as an excuse to get out of spending time with him. *Well, so what if he does know*, she thought, trying to ignore the guilt snaking through her brain. *It's not as if I care what he thinks.*

But it was nice of him to offer to help, a small voice said in her head.

Amy ignored it. "Here's a grooming kit," she said. "Could you groom Rosie and Jake for me — the Appaloosa filly and the Clydesdale," she explained.

Tim nodded. "Their halters?" he said.

"Hanging outside their stalls," Amy replied. She frowned. "Maybe I'd better put Rosie's on — she came here to be cured of being headshy and although she's getting better, she's only used to being haltered by me or Ty at the moment."

"Well, if you think she's ready, I don't mind having a go,"

Tim offered, looking at Rosie. "She's going to have to get used to other people handling her as well. Why not let me have a try?"

Every fibre in Amy's being wanted to object. Heartland was hers – and her mom's – she didn't want to let her father have anything to do with it. But how could she say that?

"I'm not going to get worried if she goes up in the air or anything," Tim said.

"OK," Amy reluctantly agreed, unable to think of an excuse.

They walked over to the stall. As usual, Rosie's head was lowered, her eyes half-closed. "Is she OK?" Tim said.

"Yeah, she always stands like that," Amy said, her apprehension at her father handling Rosie making her almost curt.

"She doesn't look right to me," Tim said.

"She's fine," Amy answered.

Tim looked as if he was about to say something more but then he seemed to change his mind. "Sorry," he said. "Of course you know your own horses best."

Amy nodded but inside she felt a twinge of guilt. She couldn't deny that, much as she told herself that Rosie's quietness was just a personality trait, a feeling was still niggling her that something wasn't quite right with the filly.

Tim took the halter off the door and went into the stall. Rosie backed off as he entered. "Hi there, girl," Tim said softly. "You're a beauty, aren't you?" He didn't approach the filly, but waited until she came to him.

With a snort, Rosie bent her head and snuffled at his hands.

"Now, let's see about this halter," Tim said. Murmuring to her in a soft voice, he drew the noseband of the halter slowly but confidently over the filly's chestnut muzzle and fastened the strap behind her ears.

Amy tensed, waiting for an explosion, but none came. Rosie flinched slightly but stood still. "There's a good girl," Tim praised. He turned to Amy. "And you say she used to be badly headshy?"

Amy nodded.

"Then you've done an amazing job," Tim said.

Amy felt a wave of pride but she squashed it firmly. *You don't care what he thinks*, she reminded herself firmly. "I'd better go and get on with the rest of the grooming," she said, and hurried away.

Amy groomed Sundance and then went to find Lou to see if she could give her a hand turning Blackjack and Crispin out. But Lou was nowhere to be found. Feeling puzzled, Amy asked Ty if he knew where she was.

"She said something about getting on with some work in the office," Ty said.

Amy went down to the house. Why would Lou be working in the office when their father was out on the yard? Surely Lou would want to spend as much time with him as possible? But Ty was right. Lou was sitting in the office, her laptop open in front of her.

"What are you doing in here, Lou?" Amy said, in surprise.

"Working, of course," Lou said shortly.

"But what about Daddy?" Amy said.

"What about him?" Lou said. "He seems happy enough helping you."

Her tone was unmistakably abrupt. Amy frowned. "What's up?"

"Nothing," Lou said. She saw Amy raise her eyebrows. "Look, Ty said there wasn't that much to do so I thought I'd come in here and get the business plan finished. That's all," she said. "There's nothing up. I'll see you and Daddy when you're done with the horses." She turned back to her laptop and began typing, clearly signalling that the conversation was over.

Amy hesitated. Despite Lou's denial, it was obvious that something had put her sister in a bad mood. However, she wasn't about to share what it was, so, with a shrug, Amy went back outside.

A little while later, Amy began to work Rosie in the school. She wanted to see if she could get to the bottom of the filly's headshaking. So far, neither she nor Ty had been able to work out what was causing it. As usual, Amy started the session by sending Rosie round the ring and joining-up with her.

She was just walking round the ring with the filly following at her shoulder when she looked up and saw Tim watching from the gate. "That was amazing to watch," he said. "It's called joining-up, isn't it?"

"Yes," Amy said, shocked that he'd heard of it.

He seemed to see her surprise. "I saw a guy doing it last year when I was over in England," he explained. "I've got a couple of two-year-olds at home and I'm planning to try it when I break them in next year." He smiled. "I was just talking to Ty about some of the other therapies you use here. It sounds like you do a really great job," he said, smiling warmly. "Taking on horses with problems, curing and rehoming them – it's a pity there aren't more places in the world like Heartland."

Amy felt torn. She so wanted to hate him, but how could she, when he said things like that?

Tim looked at Rosie. "So, how have you conquered her headshyness?"

Amy seized gratefully on the subject of the horse and explained. "I'll show you," she finished.

Rosie was now so confident around Amy that she would let her do almost anything to her ears, but there was still one spot just near the scar that she was didn't like being handled. As she backed away, Amy sent her out round the ring. Ten minutes later, the filly was standing letting Amy stroke her scar.

It was only then that Amy took her concentration off Rosie to look across at her father to see if he understood. "See?"

Tim nodded. "Yeah, I do. I use the same principles when I'm training – reward the behaviour you want, ignore the behaviour you don't. I used them when I was showjumping too."

He seemed to see the surprised expression on Amy's face. "Why? Did you think I used to beat my horses over the fences?" As her face flushed guiltily, he shook his head. "Amy, you knew Pegasus. Can you imagine how far I'd have got if I'd tried to use force with him?" He shook his head. "That was one amazing horse. If you asked him to do something he'd try his heart out for you, but if you tried to force him –" he smiled a faint smile – "well, you'd more than likely end up on the floor."

"He was always like that," Amy said, feeling the back of her eyes suddenly welling up with tears, "right till the end."

Tim cleared his throat. "So ... how did he die?" he said. "I mean, I know you said it was cancer, but what happened?"

"It was after Mom's accident." Amy swallowed. "He ... he was fine for a few months, and then it was like he realized she wasn't coming back. He stopped eating and eventually he just got too weak and ... and –" she took a deep breath – "we had to put him down." Blinking her tears back, she looked at her father. His face was full of emotion.

Tim rubbed a hand over his forehead. "You miss him a lot?"

Amy had to force the words past the lump in her throat. "More than I can say," she whispered painfully.

"Me too," Tim said, his eyes meeting hers. "I've missed him for twelve years."

Amy stared at him as the truth suddenly hit her. He was the one person in the world who could understand how she felt. He'd loved the great grey horse as much as she had. "I ... I could show you where he's buried, if you like," she whispered.

As soon as the words were out of her mouth she began to regret them. Pegasus's burial spot was a very special place to her. But it was too late. The offer had been made.

"Yes, I'd like that," Tim said quietly. "Thank you."

"I'll just put Rosie away, then," Amy said.

As she led the filly to one of the turn-out paddocks, her mind raced. She was about to show Pegasus's grave to her father. She reached deep inside her and tried to dredge up the anger she usually felt towards him, but it had gone.

So, how did she feel about him, then?

I don't know, she thought in confusion.

Reaching the paddock gate, she unclipped Rosie's lead-rope and the filly trotted over to the stream that ran through the field and began to graze under one of the willow trees.

"She always grazes in that spot," Amy told Tim.

He smiled. "It's amazing how horses have their favourite places to eat — maybe she thinks the grass tastes better there."

Amy half wished that they could stay there talking about Rosie, but she could sense her father's restlessness. She swallowed. There was no going back now. "Pegasus's field is over there," she said.

Chapter Eight

Tim followed her down the drive to the empty paddock. The winter's rain and lack of grazing had left the grass green. In the middle of the paddock stood a single young oak tree. It was silhouetted against the sky, fresh leaf buds bursting out on its slender branches.

Opening the gate, Amy walked over to it. At the foot of the tree was a mound of earth. Once bare soil, it now had a thin coat of grass seedlings.

Amy didn't need to say a word. Tim knelt beside the mound and touched it. For a moment, he didn't speak.

"I remember when you were tiny," he said, at last to Amy. "You refused to be left behind when your mother, Lou and I went for rides, and so I'd sit you in front of me on Pegasus. I swear he was a different horse when he knew you were on his back. Not once did he buck or carry on like he used to when I was riding on my own."

Amy nodded. "I remember he used to let me play around his feet when Mom was grooming him or working in his stall. Once I braided his tail with lots of different coloured ribbons. I couldn't wait to be big enough to groom him properly."

Tim smiled at her. "He was a horse in a million."

"The best," Amy agreed.

"So brave," Tim said. his eyes clouded with memories. "Any other horse would have refused to jump off such a tight angle but he didn't, he trusted me and he tried to do it..." He broke off, pinching the bridge of his nose.

Amy knew he'd been talking about the night of his accident – that night at the World Championships when he had turned Pegasus too sharply into a fence. Pegasus had caught the top pole between his legs and come crashing down.

Tim took in a deep breath. "It doesn't matter how many years pass, it doesn't get any easier." He looked at her. "But he was a lucky horse to have you and your mother to look after him."

Amy didn't know what to say. Part of her wanted to shout out that he had no right to say such a thing, but at the same time, there was no denying the love and loss in her father's eyes. He saved her the need to speak by quickly squeezing her shoulder.

"I'm glad you loved him too, Amy," he said.

And, in that moment, Amy gave up her desire to fight him. Her father had loved Pegasus as much as she had and, for now, that was enough. Her eyes met his. "I did," she whispered. "I still do."

They stood side by side, each looking at the grave, their love for Pegasus wrapping around them, drawing them together.

Tim crouched down. "Sleep well, old friend," he whispered, touching the grassy mound. "You deserve it."

After a long moment, he stood up. "Well," he said, his tone lightening. "I guess I shouldn't hold you up any longer. Not when there's still so much to do."

Amy glanced at him. The hint of a smile was flickering at the corners of her father's mouth. Almost before she realized what she was doing, she had smiled back. "I think we'll manage," she admitted, rather sheepishly.

"You know, I meant what I said yesterday," Tim said as they walked back across the paddock together, "I would love to go out for a ride."

"Well, we can," Amy said, shutting the gate behind them. "We could go after lunch."

"Do you think there's any point in trying to persuade Lou to come with us?" Tim said.

Amy shook her head.

Tim sighed. "She used to love horses – and riding – so much."

"Not any more," Amy said.

Her father seemed to catch the slight note of wistfulness in her voice. "And that causes a problem between you?"

Amy hesitated. Although she felt a whole load closer to

her father than she had done at the start of the day, she didn't want to discuss Lou and her attitudes towards horses with him. Amy felt that whatever she said would feel like a betrayal of her sister. "Not really," she lied. She quickly moved the conversation in a different direction. "So ... er ... what did you think of Rosie?" she asked, as they approached the paddock in which the Appaloosa filly was turned out. She was still in the same place by the stream, but now instead of grazing she was nibbling the bare arching branches of the willow tree.

She felt her father look at her for a moment, but then he went along with the change of subject. "You've done a wonderful job on her," he said, studying the filly. "To go from not wanting to be haltered, to behaving as well as she did today — and in just a week — well, that's a fantastic achievement." As he spoke, Rosie lifted her head and circled it in the air. Tim frowned. "I don't like that head-shaking though — you're going to have to sort that out. And there's something else, I can't put my finger on it. Maybe it's her quietness, but something doesn't seem quite right with her."

Though Amy felt slightly put out at the less-than-complete praise, deep down she was glad her father was being honest about what he thought. She knew that she would never lie about her opinion of a horse just to make someone feel better, and it made her respect her father more, realizing that he wouldn't either. "I know," she admitted. "I guess I've sort of been feeling the same myself."

"Have you had her checked over by a vet?" Tim asked, stopping at the fence and looking at the filly.

"Yes, she was examined by a vet before she came here," Amy replied. "He gave her the all-clear but the next day, when her owner tried to put the halter on, Rosie reared up in the stable and hit her head on the wooden partition. After that, she became totally impossible to halter and that's when we were contacted."

Tim frowned. "Maybe she did herself some damage when she reared up. That was after the vet's visit, right?" Amy nodded. "You say her behaviour got worse after that — perhaps she injured herself then."

Of course! Amy stared at him. Why hadn't she thought of that? "That could explain why she's been shaking her head!" she exclaimed. "And why she's been so quiet."

"She could have a small fracture," Tim said. He frowned suddenly. "You know what, I bet that's a basket willow she's chewing." He started to climb the fence.

"Basket willow?" Amy echoed, climbing after him.

Tim strode across the field, only slowing down as he reached the filly. "I knew it!" he said, examining the tree. "Basket willow," he said, turning to Amy. "It's a natural pain-killer. Horses graze on it when they're in pain." He saw her surprised expression. "Don't tell me your mom didn't teach you that?"

"No, she didn't," Amy replied. "How do you know about it?"

"An old horseman told me about it," Tim replied. He patted Rosie who was snuffling hopefully at his pockets. "Poor girl. I reckon you've got a headache." His fingers stroked gently up her face, examining the bones on either side. When he reached a spot just above her left eye, Rosie tossed her head. Tim tried again but every time his fingers reached the same spot, Rosie threw her head in the air. "Yeah, there's definitely something bothering her," Tim said. "If I were you I'd get her checked over again."

Amy nodded. "I'll ring Scott." She stroked the Appaloosa's nose. "We'll find out what's wrong with you, girl. I promise."

When Amy telephoned Scott, he agreed to call round the next morning. "My dad thinks Rosie might have a small fracture," Amy said. My dad. Suddenly she realized that it was the first time in his visit that she had said those two words aloud. It felt strange to say them – strange but good, she decided. She caught Tim's eye and realized that the words hadn't escaped him either. He was smiling at her.

"I wish you were staying longer," she said impulsively, as she replaced the receiver.

"Well, I'm here for a week," Tim said. "I've got business to attend to, and then I fly back on Saturday night. I could come and visit some more. I'd have suggested it from the start, but I thought it might be best to see how the weekend went first. But if you'd like me to visit in the afternoons when I've finished with work, then I'd love to."

Lou came into the kitchen.

"Lou," Amy said quickly. "Daddy's going to come and visit each day this week."

"That's nice," Lou said, but there was a strangely flat note in her voice.

"Amy's just been showing me Pegasus's field," Tim said.

Lou stared at Amy. Amy understood her astonishment. Lou knew how special Pegasus's grave was to her. Amy wished she could explain how Tim understood and shared her love for Pegasus – shared it in a way that no one else could. But with him standing there, she couldn't put those thoughts into words.

"And I watched a join-up," Tim went on. "It was fantastic." He looked proudly at Amy. "Amy's got a real gift with horses."

Happiness flooded through Amy. "I'm not the only one." She turned to Lou. "Daddy's helped me work out what's causing Rosie to shake her head. We think she's injured it."

"Well, I'm glad that you think you've got the problem sorted out," Lou said abruptly.

The tension in Lou's voice was obvious. Amy frowned. What was the matter with her? Wondering if Lou was feeling a bit left out, she turned to Tim. "Lou noticed the head-shaking before any of us," she said, wanting to include Lou. "The first day I worked Rosie, she saw it. And she noticed that Rosie seemed quiet."

"Well, it looks like your instincts were probably right,

Lou." Tim smiled at her. "Now, Amy and I have decided to go out riding this afternoon," he went on. "Why don't you join us?"

But Lou shook her head. "I'm busy. I want to get this business plan finished so Grandpa and Amy can see it tonight. In fact," she cleared her throat, "I think I'd better go and do some more work on it right now."

And, looking at the floor, she hurried out of the room.

Amy frowned. Something was up with her — but what?

Amy and Tim took Moochie and Sundance out along one of the trails in the woods behind Heartland that afternoon. As they rode up the mountain, Tim talked about his business importing and exporting young sports horses to and from Australia.

"I love it," he told her, his eyes gleaming. "You take a shaggy-coated, unbacked three-year-old that a buyer wouldn't look twice at and, twelve months down the line, you've got a fit, well-mannered young horse."

"Do you back them yourself?" Amy asked.

"No, the old injury to my neck won't stand too much falling off," Tim said. "But I supervise. I've got a staff of ten." He smiled. "You'll have to come and visit."

"I'd like to," Amy said, smiling at him. She saw a fallen tree-trunk on the track ahead and shortened her reins. "Watch Sundance jump this!"

Sundance flew over the log.

"What do you think?" Amy said, cantering up to Moochie.

Tim was shaking his head. "You're so like your mother," he said. "Watching you ride is like seeing her all over again."

Amy reined Sundance in. *Like Mom. He thinks I'm like Mom*, she thought. No compliment could have been better.

She glanced across at him. His eyes were warm and suddenly a question burst from her. "Why did you leave us?"

As soon as the word left her lips she felt the blood rush to her cheeks and she looked down at Sundance's mane feeling very embarrassed.

For a moment, there was a silence and then she heard Tim sigh. "Cowardice, weakness," he said quietly. "I just couldn't cope. You have to remember that at the time no one could even be sure if I would ever walk again, and my career as a showjumper was over. I'd always been so strong, so fit. I felt that your mother would be better off without me, that if she stayed with me, it would be out of pity. And that was something I couldn't handle – that's why I left."

"Disappeared," Amy said, trying but failing to keep the accusatory tone out of her voice.

Tim's eyes met hers. "Do you think I could have gone if I'd stayed to say goodbye? Amy, you, your mother, Lou – you were the three most precious things in the world to me. There's no way that I could have looked at your faces and then turned and walked away."

"You shouldn't have gone!" Amy protested. "Mom would have stayed with you – not out of pity, but out of love."

"I realized that in the end — that's when I got back in touch with your mother to beg her for a reconciliation," Tim said. "But by then it was too late. I had hurt her too badly." He shook his head, his face showing self-disgust. "I'd always prided myself on being brave. But the moment when I needed courage it failed me. I took the coward's way out and ran away. It's a decision that will haunt me for the rest of my life."

Amy felt the anger leave her. "You've got Helena now," she said. "And Lily."

"Yes," Tim said, his eyes growing warm. "I have."

Amy swallowed, wondering suddenly about the woman who had taken her mom's place. "What's Helena like?" she asked, trying to keep her voice casual.

If she was hoping for her dad to say not as perfect as her mom she was disappointed. "Wonderful," Tim said. "It was Helena who made me realize that I couldn't let the mistakes I'd made in the past wreck the rest of my life. That I had to accept what had happened and move on — just like your mother had done." He smiled. "I knew she would understand. When we were together she always used to say it was a waste of time to regret what had happened in the past — learn, move on and—"

"Look to the good times ahead," Amy finished quietly. It was a saying that she knew well.

"That's right. Well, it's what I've tried to do. And —" Tim's eyes met hers — "what I'm going to try and do from now on."

* * *

"You look like you've had a good time," Ty commented, as Amy put Sundance away in his stall, half an hour later.

"The best!" Amy said.

"So maybe your dad isn't so bad, after all?" Ty said, coming into the stall.

"Absolutely," Amy said. She put an arm over Sundance's back and smiled radiantly. "It's like all these questions in my mind have finally been answered. I understand at last. And not just that. He understands me. I feel like –" she looked at Ty to see if he knew what she was getting at – "well... like I belong."

"That's awesome, Amy," Ty said and before Amy knew what was happening he had bent his head and was brushing her lips with his own.

Amy kissed him back and sighed happily. It was the perfect end to a perfect afternoon.

At six-thirty, Jack's car drew up in front of the house. Amy and Lou both went to meet him.

"How was your weekend, Grandpa?" Lou asked.

"Great," Jack said. "But more importantly –" his eyes searched their faces – "how was yours?"

"Fine," Lou said. "It was fine." There was a slight hesitation in her voice.

Jack frowned. "But not like you'd hoped?"

"It was just fine," Lou said quickly. "Wasn't it, Amy?"

"Yeah," Amy said. "It was..." she was about to say awesome, but stopped herself. She didn't want to hurt Grandpa's feelings by going on about how great it had been to see Daddy. "It was OK," she said. "And, well —" she looked nervously at Grandpa, wondering how he'd react to what she was about to tell him — "Daddy's going to come and visit this week — after he's finished work each day."

Grandpa's mouth tightened and, for a moment, he went very quiet. "Well, if it makes you both happy, I'm glad," he said, at last.

Amy knew how hard it must have been for him to say those words. "It does," she said gratefully. "Doesn't it, Lou?"

"Of course," Lou said lightly. "Now, Grandpa," she said, changing the subject. "Come inside. I've finished the business plan and when you've had a chance to relax I'd really like to go through it with you and Amy. Then I can take it into the bank tomorrow — if you both agree to it, of course," she added quickly. "We need to get the bid in as quickly as possible — before the Grants, at least."

They went into the house. Grandpa got changed and then came down to the kitchen where Amy was helping Lou prepare some pasta for supper.

"OK, let's have a look at this plan, then," he said, sitting down at the table.

Amy added the remaining ingredients to the bolognese sauce and then, leaving it to simmer on the stove, she sat down beside him.

Lou handed each of them a copy of the business plan. "If you have a look through it, then we can discuss it," she said.

Amy ran her eyes over the paper. There were lots of figures. Initial outlay, overheads, net profit. The words spun through her brain.

"You can see it's going to be profitable," Lou said, after a few minutes. "And it could bring in a regular income, which is exactly what we need to support Amy's rehabilitation work." Her eyes shone. "If it turns out to be a success then it could fund extensions to Heartland – we might have another barn, another training ring. We could do so much more to help."

Amy bit her lip. On paper she could see that there were no arguments. It did sound like a good idea.

"It's a big risk, Lou," Jack said, looking down the plan to the money they would have to borrow.

"Yes, but risks are all part of a good business plan," Lou said. She looked at him. "It will work, Grandpa," she said. "It really will."

"All right," Jack said slowly. "If Amy agrees, then you can submit the plan."

Both he and Lou looked at Amy.

"Well?" Lou asked her hopefully.

Amy took a deep breath. She didn't want to upset Lou at such a difficult time. "OK," she said extremely reluctantly. "I agree."

The look that crossed Lou's face almost made the sacrifice worth it.

"It's the right decision, Amy," Lou said, in delight. "You just wait and see!"

Chapter Nine

"So how did Ben do at the show?" Soraya said to Amy on the bus the next morning on the way to school.

"He won his class," Amy told her. "He was thrilled."

"Cool!" Soraya said. She grinned. "Maybe I'll have to come over and congratulate him."

Amy grinned back. "And suggest he takes you out for a victory dinner?"

"Of course," Soraya said, arching her eyebrows. "I mean, it's the perfect excuse." She smiled. "Well, apart from the riding-school plan it sounds like you had a pretty cool weekend."

"I did," Amy said, her eyes glowing with the memory. "It was so good seeing my dad and talking to him at last."

"And he's coming to visit all week?" Soraya said.

"Every day," Amy replied.

"What did your grandpa say when he found out?" Soraya asked. "I bet he wasn't exactly delighted."

"Well," Amy admitted, "I think he wishes Daddy had just stayed away."

"It must be really hard for him," Soraya said. "What about Lou? She must be pleased."

"If she is, she's got a funny way of showing it," Amy said. She saw Soraya's intrigued expression and shook her head. "She was in a totally odd mood yesterday. It was almost like she was avoiding Daddy. When he was helping on the yard she just went and worked inside. I thought she'd be pleased that I was getting on so well with him, but she seemed almost angry."

"Maybe she was feeling a bit left out," Soraya suggested. "I mean, if you and your dad were talking horses quite a bit, well, that's not really Lou's thing, is it?"

Amy frowned. "I kind of wondered that too." She thought about the weekend. "I guess we did talk about horsey things a lot." Suddenly she remembered the argument between Lou and Tim on Saturday. "Dad's got this theory that Lou won't ride because she's scared."

"Do you think he's right?" Soraya asked.

"Well, Lou says she isn't scared, and she certainly doesn't act scared around the horses, but it is odd that she won't ride." Amy's eyes widened. "Perhaps that's why she's avoiding Daddy — she is scared and she's worried he'll make her admit it."

Soraya grinned. "Careful, Amy. You're in danger of becoming a human psychologist as well as a horse one."

"But I could be right," Amy said.

Just then Matt got on the bus and Amy dropped the subject. Since Matt had started going out with Ashley, she had felt weird talking about personal stuff when he was around.

"How was your weekend?" Soraya asked him as he sat down.

"Not that great," Matt replied. He sighed. "I broke up with Ashley."

Amy and Soraya both stared at him. "You dumped Ashley?" Amy exclaimed.

"Yeah," Matt said heavily. "She kept trying to run my life. It was like I didn't have a life outside dating her."

"Wow!" Amy said, impressed. "No one ever dumps Ashley."

"She did seem to take it kind of hard," Matt said quietly.

"And how are you about it?" Soraya asked him, her brown eyes concerned.

"I'm fine," Matt muttered.

"You are so much better off without her," Amy said. "Ow!" she exclaimed as Soraya elbowed her sharply. She glared at her friend but Soraya was looking at Matt's face

"You really liked her, didn't you, Matt?" Soraya said softly.

"Yeah, I reckon I did," Matt admitted, and for the first time, Amy took in the sadness in his eyes. He sighed. "I know you two don't get on with her, but she's not as bad as she seems — really she's not. When you get her on her own, she's just normal, vulnerable even. She hasn't had it easy, you know — right from when she was little her mom had her riding in shows every weekend..."

"My heart bleeds for her," Amy said sarcastically. "Come on. I helped my mom with the horses from when I could barely walk!"

"Don't be so harsh, Amy — your mom never treated you like a performing doll," Matt said and Amy immediately felt bad. "Ashley's always had to look good, win ribbons, get her photo in the papers," Matt went on. "That was what her mom and dad expected and so that's what she did."

Amy didn't say anything. OK, maybe Ashley hadn't had it totally easy, but she still had a major attitude problem. However, she could see that Matt was upset and so she didn't say anything. She squeezed his arm. "You did the right thing," she said comfortingly. "You couldn't have let her boss you around."

"I know," Matt said. He shook his head. "I just wish I didn't feel so bad."

When Amy got back to Heartland that afternoon, Tim had already arrived. He was helping Ty groom Jake. "Hey, there!" he called as she walked up the drive.

That's my dad, Amy thought, looking at him, his jeans dusty, a grooming brush in his hand. It was weird seeing him doing stuff at Heartland — but a good sort of weird.

"Hi," she said, going over. "You're here early."

"I finished work sooner than I expected," Tim said. "So I came over to see if I could lend a hand."

"We've been busy," Ty said. "Scott X-rayed Rosie after lunch."

"Did he find anything?" Amy asked quickly.

"Yeah, a hairline fracture just above one eye," Ty replied. "It'll heal on its own but while it does he's given us some painkillers for her. I suggested that we feed her comfrey to speed up the healing and he agreed. We should massage around the area with lavender oil to help relax her and ease her headache, but we need to be careful to avoid the exact spot."

"Have you told Sheri?" Amy asked.

"Yeah, she was really pleased that we'd found out what the matter was. Scott said that the fracture should heal fairly quickly so she should be able to start working Rosie in about a month," Ty said.

"Great," Amy said, feeling a huge weight roll off her mind. Rosie still had to get better but at least they knew what the problem was now. "Where's Lou, and Grandpa?"

"Jack's out," Tim replied. "Lou's inside working."

"Oh, right," Amy said. "I'll go get changed."

She walked towards the house, wondering whether her suspicions of that morning were true. Was Lou avoiding Daddy because she was scared of riding?

She found her sister sitting at the kitchen table with the account books and her laptop open in front of her.

"What are you doing in here?" Amy asked.

"What does it look like?" Lou said shortly. "I'm working."

"But I thought you'd finished the business plan," Amy said. "Didn't you say you were going to drop it in at the bank this morning?"

"Yes, and I did," Lou said. "But I've been so busy I've got really behind with the accounts." She ran a hand through her hair. "And I'm not going to catch up if you stand here chattering to me."

"Sorry for breathing," Amy muttered, heading for her room, but just before she reached the door, she stopped. She had to say something. "Lou, I don't get it," she said. "I thought you'd be pleased that Daddy was here. I thought you'd want to spend as much time with him as possible."

"I do," Lou said, but Amy had caught the moment's hesitation before she spoke. "But there's still work to do." Lou bent her head over her laptop. "I'll see Daddy when I'm done."

Amy spoke impulsively. "Is it because you're —" She broke off, suddenly remembering how touchy Lou had been when Tim had asked her whether she was scared. She and Lou had been getting on quite well. Did she really want to start an argument with her now?

"Because I'm what?" Lou said, looking up with a frown.

Amy hesitated for a moment, and then shook her head. "It doesn't matter," she said, deciding against pursuing her question. She headed for the stairs. "I'm going to get changed."

* * *

As Amy pulled on her old jeans she remembered that she'd been going to ring Mrs Newhart to ask if Jo could ride Feather. She went through to the office and picked up the phone. Her mouth felt dry. She wasn't really looking forward to the conversation, but Ty was right, they needed to find out how Feather would behave with Jo.

Donna Newhart answered.

Amy quickly explained why she was ringing. "He's been really good since he got here," she said. "He hasn't done a thing wrong. I'm as sure as I can be that he's safe."

There was a silence from Mrs Newhart's end of the phone.

"Mrs Newhart?" Amy said, at last.

"OK," Mrs Newhart agreed reluctantly. "If you think he's safe, then Jo-Ann can ride him." A note of pleading entered her voice. "But please – don't let anything happen to her."

Half an hour later, Jo came walking up the drive. "I can't believe Mom said I can actually ride Feather again!" she exclaimed, dumping her bike and racing over to where Amy was grooming Rosie. "Can I go and tack him up right now?"

"OK," Amy said, with a smile.

Within ten minutes, Jo had her helmet on and was riding Feather around the ring.

"He looks fine," Tim said to Amy, as they watched together from the gate.

"I know," Amy said, looking at the pretty Arabian pony.

"He's been like this ever since he got here — not a hint of him playing up."

"Perhaps something just spooked him that day you saw him," Tim suggested.

Amy thought back and frowned. "He didn't look as if there was anything he was afraid of," she said, remembering how Feather had slowed down and tried to pull to the gate before he had finally reared."

"Well, he looks great now," Tim commented, as Jo moved Feather into a smooth trot.

"Yeah," Amy said. She knew she'd have felt better if it had been something that she'd done that had brought about his improvement. OK, they'd used T-Touch on him and massaged him with violet-leaf oil, but that was all. She looked at the grey pony as he trotted around the ring. *He is better, I'm certain he is*, she told herself, wishing she could shake off the slight doubt that lingered in her mind.

The next morning, Matt wasn't on the bus on the way to school. However, as Amy and Soraya made their way to their first class, he came jogging up behind them. "Hi, guys!" he said. "Scott gave me a lift in."

Compared to the day before, he sounded really cheerful. Amy looked at him in surprise. "You look happy."

Matt grinned. "Ashley rang me last night. She said she's totally sorry for the way she treated me and that she'd like to give our relationship another go."

Amy and Soraya stared at him. "You didn't say yes, did you?" Amy said.

"Sure did," Matt said. "It's going to be fine," he said quickly, seeing their faces. "Ashley promised she won't boss me around any more."

Amy saw a faint blush creeping up his neck. "And what else did she say?"

Matt shrugged, but was unable to keep the pleased grin off his face. "Oh, just some other stuff – about how I'm not like the other boys she's dated." He looked at them pleadingly. "Come on, you guys, be happy for me."

Soraya sighed. "OK, I guess we'll try."

As Amy was walking home from the bus stop, Lou's car came along the road. She stopped and opened the door. "Jump in," she said. "I'll give you a lift."

Amy chucked her back-pack into the well of the passenger seat and got in.

"So, how's your day been?" Lou asked, as they set off up the drive.

"OK – apart from the fact that Matt's dating Ashley again," Amy replied. "I don't know what he sees in her." She shook her head, not wanting to think about it. "Have you heard from the bank yet?"

"No," Lou replied. "But we shouldn't have to wait too long, although we've still got a fight against Green Briar to get the land."

She parked the car and they went into the kitchen together.

Grandpa was speaking on the phone. "OK," he was saying, "I'll tell them." His voice was terse, and he put the phone down without saying goodbye.

Amy frowned. "Who was that?" she asked.

Jack's face looked strained. "Your father," he said. "He can't make it here tonight. He has to see some clients."

"Oh," Amy said, feeling disappointed. Without saying another word, Jack strode out of the room. Amy sighed. "I wish Grandpa could get along better with Daddy." Although Jack hadn't gone out the day before when Tim had been visiting, he had stayed in the house and avoided any contact with his former son-in-law.

"I think that might be too much to ask," Lou said. "It's putting a real strain on him — having Daddy here all week."

There was a strange note in Lou's voice. Amy frowned. It almost sounded as if Lou was accusing her of not considering Grandpa's feelings. "You were the one who invited Daddy here in the first place, Lou!" she protested.

"I know," Lou said defensively. "I'm just saying that it's tough on Grandpa." She pushed her fingers through her hair. "You know, maybe we shouldn't have asked Daddy to come and visit us every day."

Amy was astonished. Was this Lou speaking? The Lou who had refused to rest until she had got in contact with their father again. "I don't get you, Lou," she said. "You were the one who was desperate to see Daddy again, but now he's here, you don't seem very happy."

"Of course I'm happy," Lou said quickly, heading for the stairs.

"No, you're not!" Amy said, in exasperation. "Lou — what's wrong?"

For a moment, she thought her sister was just going to ignore her, but then Lou stopped.

"I don't know," she said, in a voice so quiet that Amy could hardly hear her. Her shoulders sagged as she turned back. "It's just —" she seemed to be struggling to find the right words — "just that Daddy's visit isn't turning out like I imagined. We don't seem to have anything to say to each other any more."

"You've just got to get to know him again," Amy said. "Spend time with him."

"How can I when —" Lou broke off. "It doesn't matter," she said quickly. "Forget it."

"Lou…" Amy began, stepping towards her in concern.

Lou shook her head and backed off. "I'm going to my room," she said, and, with that, she hurried out of the door.

Amy stood there for a long moment and then slowly went upstairs herself. Grandpa's bedroom door was shut, and so was Lou's.

Amy sank down on her bed and buried her head in her hands. *I just want everyone to get along*, she thought in frustration. She sighed. Yeah, like that was really going to happen.

The atmosphere didn't improve. Lou seemed to grow more distant from their father with every day that passed, and Grandpa continued to avoid him. The only good thing, as far as Amy was concerned, was that Feather continued to behave, and on Friday, she decided that she would invite Mrs Newhart to come and watch Jo riding him that weekend.

"At least if she sees him behaving then it might make her feel happier about Jo riding him," Amy said to Tim, as they rode Solo and Sundance back from the trails that afternoon.

As they dismounted, Lou's Honda came up the drive.

She jumped out. Her eyes were shining and her face was split by a huge grin. "We've got a letter from the bank!" she cried, waving an envelope excitedly. "They've agreed to lend us the money!"

"Oh." Amy could see from Lou's sudden frown that this wasn't the reaction her sister had been wanting. "That's great, Lou." She made herself smile. "Really great," she added, trying to sound as if she meant it.

"Well done, Lou," Tim said. "You put in a lot of work on that plan."

"As soon as Grandpa signs the agreement, I can put in an offer on the land," Lou said. "This will mean we'll have a regular income. We won't just be scraping by any more — we'll be able to plan for the future. It will be brilliant for Heartland."

"I really hope so," Tim said.

The smile left Lou's face. "You ... you don't think it is?"

"Well, I don't think that you should rush into it," Tim said cautiously. "After all, it could really change things round here."

Amy saw a look of hurt flash through Lou's eyes. "Yes — for the better!"

"Lou," Tim began placatingly. "I'm just saying you should give it some careful thought."

"I've done that!" Lou snapped. "And I know it's a good idea!"

Just then, Grandpa came out of the house. It was clear that he had heard the raised voices. "What's going on?" he asked, taking in the scene.

Lou didn't answer. She marched past him but not before Amy had caught the glint of tears in her eyes.

From the look that Grandpa shot Tim, it was obvious that he had seen them too. "I don't know what you said to her," he said advancing angrily on the younger man, "but I'm not going to stand by and see you upset my granddaughter." He glared at him icily. "I want you to leave now!"

"No!" Amy protested, grabbing her father's arm. "Don't go."

"I think it might be for the best, Amy," Tim said quietly. "I don't want to cause problems for anyone. I'll call you."

"Grandpa!" Amy said, turning to him beseechingly. "Daddy didn't mean to upset Lou. All he said was that she should think carefully before making a decision that would change things round here. Lou just got all mad. It wasn't Daddy's fault!"

She saw the anger slowly fade from Grandpa's eyes. "I see," he said. He paused. "Very well, then, Tim, if you were just trying to help Lou consider the outcome of adding a riding school to Heartland then I –" he took a deep breath – "I apologize for overreacting. I guess I'm rather on edge at the moment."

Tim shook his head. "There's no need to apologize, Jack. I know you just want to protect Lou and Amy, and, believe me, I'm grateful for that. It's just I've had experience with riding schools and I know how difficult it can be to make them profitable." He rubbed his temples. "Still, I accept it's not my place to give advice. I should have kept my reservations to myself."

The tension left Grandpa's shoulders. "No," he said. "You were right to say what you thought. Relationships should be built on honesty."

"I know," Tim replied. "I want to rebuild my relationship with my daughters with honesty and trust. And..." His gaze met Grandpa's. "It would really mean a lot to me to know that I had your support, Jack."

Amy looked at Grandpa. He hesitated for a moment, but then he nodded. "You have."

"Thank you," Tim said quietly. "That means a lot."

Amy felt a wave of relief. Although Grandpa wasn't declaring friendship for her father, maybe the first step towards a reconciliation had been made.

"And now, I think I've got some more apologizing to do," Tim said, looking towards the house.

Chapter Ten

Lou was in the kitchen setting the table. Amy watched each plate hit the table-top with a bang.

"Lou, I'm sorry," Tim said, going over to her. "I should have realized how much this riding school idea means to you, and I should have been more supportive. I just wanted you to think things over before rushing into making an offer."

"I have thought things over," Lou said through gritted teeth.

"Fair enough," Tim shook his head. "Come on, Lou," he said gently. "Please don't let's argue. I've only got one more day left."

Lou walked across the room and hesitated for a while. She moved over to the window and stood looking out for a couple of moments. Amy and Tim waited quietly for her to say something. Lou sighed and turned around. "OK, you're right," she said. "I'm sorry for storming off like that. It's just I'm sure that having a riding school will be a good move for Heartland."

"I know," Tim said. For a moment, Amy thought he was going to put his arm around Lou, but then something seemed to stop him. "So ... when will you put the offer in?" he asked.

"I'll ring the Youngs now," Lou said. She glanced at Jack who was standing by the door. "That is OK, isn't it, Grandpa?"

Grandpa nodded and he, Amy and Tim sat down while Lou went to the office to phone. Amy chewed a jagged nail on her little finger. She couldn't believe that the whole riding-school thing was actually going to happen. Heartland was going to change so much.

At last, Lou came back into the room.

"Well, what did they say?" Amy demanded, seeing that her sister's face wore a look of concern.

"They've already had an offer," Lou said.

"It's Green Briar, I know it is!" Amy burst out.

"The Youngs wouldn't say who it was from," Lou said, "but I'm sure you're right. I upped *our* offer, so now we've got to just wait and see. We can't afford to go any higher."

"When will we know?" Jack asked.

"Within the next twenty-four hours," Lou said.

* * *

Although the next day was officially Ty's day off, he turned up in the morning as usual to help feed the horses and muck out the stalls. He could only stay for a few hours, though, because he had arranged to do the grocery shopping for his mom.

Tim came over to say goodbye. "It was really good to meet you, Ty," he said warmly. "I appreciate you sharing your knowledge with me this week."

"Likewise," Ty said with a smile. "I won't forget about basket willow in a hurry." He glanced at Amy. "Call me tonight?"

She nodded. Although he didn't say it out loud she knew he meant her to call after her father had gone to let him know how she was feeling. "I will."

Ty got into his truck and Amy and her father watched him drive away.

"Nice guy," Tim said, shooting a sideways look at her.

Amy smiled. "Yes," she agreed. "He is."

"So what's there to do?" Tim asked as they turned to walk back up the yard.

"Finish the stalls, tidy the muck-heap, sweep the yard, the barn, the feed-room..." Amy began to list the jobs.

Tim smiled. "I get the picture. Fetch me a broom."

At eleven o'clock, Mrs Newhart arrived. "Jo, your mom's here!" Amy called down the barn aisle to where Jo, who had been there a couple of hours, was grooming Feather.

"Oh no," Jo groaned.

"You've got nothing to worry about," Amy said briskly. "Get Feather tacked up and take him up to the ring, but don't get on him until I'm there." She hoped that having something definite to do would calm Jo's nerves.

Stowing her broom in the rack, Amy headed down the yard. Lou had come out of the kitchen and was talking to Jo's mother. As Amy approached them she saw that Mrs Newhart's face was tense. "I wish I knew what to do for the best," Amy heard her saying to Lou. "If anything was to happen to Jo-Ann then I'd never forgive myself." She shook her head. "I wish she wouldn't ride, but how can I stop her? She loves horses so much."

"It's really difficult." Amy heard a note of real sympathy in her sister's voice. "It must be awful for you."

"It is." Mrs Newhart smiled gratefully at her. "You know, at all the other barns that Jo's ever ridden, they've just dismissed me as a crazy, neurotic mom, but I can't help it. After everything that's happened..." Her voice trailed off and for a moment she looked almost embarrassed.

"It's OK," Lou said gently. "I understand." She looked up and saw Amy standing there. "Is Feather ready to be ridden?" she said, her voice regaining its usual efficiency.

Amy nodded. "Jo's taken him up to the top ring."

"She's not going to get on him without us there, is she?" Mrs Newhart asked anxiously.

"No, I told her to wait for us," Amy said.

When they got to the top ring, they found Jo massaging Feather's neck with T-Touch circles but instead of standing quietly, as normal, he was side-stepping and pulling at his reins. "Hi, Mom," Jo said nervously.

"Well, are you going to get on him, then?" Amy said, going into the ring.

Jo nodded and, taking a deep breath, she pulled down the stirrups and moved round to Feather's left side to mount.

"Don't look so worried," Amy smiled at her reassuringly. She took hold of Feather's snaffle-bit to hold him still while Jo mounted.

Shooting an anxious glance at her mom, Jo put her foot in the stirrup.

"Steady, boy," Amy said as Feather side-stepped. He threw his head in the air and backed up. Jo hopped beside him, her foot still in the stirrup-iron.

"Be careful!" Mrs Newhart called.

"Stand now," Amy said soothingly to Feather. He stood for a moment, giving Jo a chance to spring into the saddle, but as she landed lightly on his back, he plunged forward. Amy hung on.

"Just walk him round," Amy said, as Jo sorted out her stirrups. "He'll soon calm down." Although she spoke confidently, inwardly she couldn't help feeling worried. Feather seemed very tense all of a sudden.

Jo touched her heels to Feather's sides. He backed up.

Amy clicked her tongue and gave him a slight slap on his flanks. "Go on!" she told him.

Feather jogged forward. Jo pulled him to a walk. "Steady now," she told him, shooting a look in her mom's direction. But Feather continued to jog and pull.

"He is going to be OK with Jo, isn't he?" Lou asked, looking worried, as Amy joined her at the gate.

"Of course," Amy said, trying to sound as if she believed it. She could see that Mrs Newhart was gripping the top rail of the gate with white knuckles.

Tim moved closer to Amy. "Jo's looking tense," he muttered, his eyes on the horse and rider.

Amy nodded. Jo's shoulders were stiff. As Feather turned the corner at the top end of the ring and began to head towards them, he crabbed sideways, his haunches coming underneath him and his head held high. "Relax, Jo!" Amy called out, as Jo tightened her grip on the reins. What was up with Feather? In the two weeks he had been at Heartland he hadn't behaved like this once. Why had he chosen today, of all days?

"Maybe you should get off, honey, and let Amy try," Mrs Newhart called.

"I'm fine, Mom," Jo said. Her face tense, she turned Feather across the centre of the ring. When he continued to pull, she shot another anxious glance at the gate.

"She's got to stop worrying about her mom and just get on with riding him," Tim said, under his breath to Amy.

It was as if his words had lit a light bulb up over Amy's head. "Of course!" she exclaimed, staring at her father. "That's it — that's what's the matter!"

"What?" Tim said, looking mystified.

But Amy didn't have time to explain. She had to get Jo off Feather before anything happened. "Jo!" she called, hurrying across the ring. Feather, had stopped, his body parallel to the gate. Jo tried to urge him on but he just shook his head and plunged towards the gate, unseating her slightly.

Amy heard Mrs Newhart gasp.

Amy desperately tried to stay calm. She wanted to shout but she knew that doing so would risk frightening Feather and right now that was the last thing she wanted. She saw Jo nudge his sides. With a snort he began to back up, his head held high.

Amy gave up trying to be calm and broke into a run. "Jo! Get off!" she cried.

Chapter Eleven

Amy was too late. Just as she shouted, Jo kicked Feather again, and he reared up, his front legs striking out into the air.

"Jo-Ann!" Mrs Newhart screamed.

For one awful moment, Amy saw Feather stagger and thought he was going to go over backwards, but then Jo threw her weight forward, and he regained his balance and landed squarely back on the ground.

In an instant Amy had moved in beside him. "Easy now," she soothed, grabbing the reins, then, seeing Mrs Newhart running across the ring towards them, she shot a look at Jo. "Are you OK?"

Jo's face was white but she nodded.

"Jo-Ann!" Mrs Newhart gasped as she ran across the ring, her court shoes sinking into the sand.

Jo scrambled off Feather's back. "Mom, please."

"Get off that horse right now," Mrs Newhart said, hugging her fiercely, her eyes full of terror and relief.

"It's OK, Mom, I'm fine," Jo said.

Mrs Newhart was almost in tears. "Enough's enough. The pony has to go."

"But Mrs Newhart," Amy said quickly. "I know what's wrong now. If you'll just give Feather another chance—"

"Another chance!" Mrs Newhart echoed, looking at her as if she was crazy. "You've got a nerve!" Her voice rose. "You told me he was safe. Jo-Ann could have been killed!"

"If you'll just let me explain—" Amy began.

But Mrs Newhart cut her off. "No!" she said furiously. "I'm through with explanations. Jo-Ann – you're not to go near that pony again!"

"Mom!" Jo protested.

But Mrs Newhart grabbed her arm. "No, Jo, I gave Feather a second chance but no more," she said, her eyes boring into her daughter's face. "I'm not prepared to let you put yourself in danger any more. You know what happened to your grandmother. I won't let a horse ruin your life too. You're coming home with me, right now."

"But—"

"I mean it, Jo-Ann," Mrs Newhart cut in furiously. "Unless you want me to ban you from even going near horses. Now get into that car!"

Jo seemed to realize that her mom was serious and,

sobbing bitterly, she ran down the yard. Her mother strode after her.

"Mrs Newhart — wait," Lou said, following them.

Amy groaned and buried her head in Feather's neck. He nuzzled her back and looking up she saw the puzzlement in his eyes. "Well, Feather," she sighed. "You've really gone and done it now." She couldn't believe she hadn't worked out what the problem was sooner. If she had only realized then the whole incident could have been prevented.

"Are you OK?" Tim's voice said.

Amy looked round. Her father was walking across the ring towards her. "No," she said.

"You can't blame yourself," Tim said softly. "You thought he was cured — everyone did."

Amy shook her head. "Deep down I think I knew that we hadn't really sorted out his problem." She kicked the sand in frustration. "If only I'd worked out what the matter was sooner, then none of this need have happened, and Jo would have been able to keep him."

"So why do you think he reared?" Tim asked.

"I'm sure it's because of Jo," Amy explained. "He's so sensitive, he's reacting to Jo's tension when she's riding in front of her mom." She shook her head. "She even told me that the only times he misbehaved were when her mom was watching, but I didn't connect that with him misbehaving. I thought it was just bad luck."

"You're right," Tim said nodding. "Jo's tense because she

knows how nervous her mom is. He picks up on that tension and starts getting upset."

"Yes, and he tries to pull to the gate to get out of the ring," Amy continued. "Then when Jo stops him, he panics because he can't escape from a situation that's frightening him and he rears." She stroked Feather. "I'm sure that's what's causing it. He's so responsive to ride – it's like he can read your mind. I'm sure he's just reacting to Jo's emotions when her mom's watching."

"Well, why don't you get on him and see?" Tim said. "If he's good with you then it will certainly point to the problem being Jo's tension."

Amy looked at him in surprise. "You'd let me – even after he just reared like that?"

"I wouldn't have thought I could prevent you," Tim said, with a wry smile. "Seriously. If I thought you were in any real danger then of course I'd try and stop you, but I agree with your theory."

Amy smiled at him and took hold of Feather's reins. "Here goes, then," she said, mounting.

Feather stood like a rock as she adjusted the stirrup leathers. Once she was ready, she squeezed his sides. He walked forward calmly. Shortening her reins, she walked, trotted and then cantered three circuits. Feather responded perfectly. To finish off, she leaned forward and galloped him down the long side of the ring. As she reached the corner she slowed him into a canter, circled him and then trotted him over to the gate.

"I'm right. I know I am!" Amy exclaimed, her face glowing.

"Well done," Tim said, looking at her proudly.

As their eyes met, a wave of emotion overwhelmed Amy. *He understands me*, she thought. *He's my father*. As the words repeated in her brain, it was as if every cell in her body started to sing. She was his daughter, and, despite the twelve years that had passed, she knew with a sudden certainty that there was a bond between them that couldn't be broken.

"Oh, Daddy," she exclaimed. "Thank you for helping me understand what was wrong."

"You called me Daddy," Tim said, looking surprised but delighted.

"That's because you are my daddy," Amy replied, her eyes shining. "And you trusted me. You helped me to see what the problem was."

"I didn't do anything," Tim said. "It was you who took the chance. You had the courage of your convictions." His grey eyes scanned her face. "Amy, you're a talented person and, although I can't expect you to care what I think, I just want to say how proud I am you're my daughter."

Amy had to force the words past the lump that was swelling in her throat. "But I do care what you think," she managed to say, her eyes brimming with tears. "I really do."

"Amy, you'll never know how much it means to me to hear you say that," Tim said.

"It's true," Amy said.

For a moment, despite the fact that she was on Feather, she thought her father was going to sweep her into his arms, but just then the sound of footsteps on the gravel path behind them made them turn.

"Lou!" Amy said.

Lou stared at her in horror. "Amy! What are you doing on Feather?" she exclaimed. "Get off!"

The good news burst from Amy. "No, it's fine! I've worked out what was wrong, Feather's safe. He was just reacting to Jo's tension. Watch." She gathered up Feather's reins and squeezed him on.

"No!" Lou gasped.

The intensity in Lou's voice made Amy bring Feather to a halt. "But he's fine."

"Get off, now!" Lou's voice rose, almost hysterically.

"It's OK, Lou," Tim said. "Amy's just been riding him. There isn't a problem."

Lou rounded on him. "I can't believe you let Amy get on him!"

"I—" Tim began.

"How could you have been so irresponsible?" Lou cried. "Amy could have been seriously injured."

"But she hasn't been," Tim said. "She—"

"So that makes it OK, does it?" Lou exclaimed, interrupting him. Shaking with emotion, she glared furiously at him. "For goodness' sake! You of all people should know how dangerous horses can be. How could you let Amy risk herself in such a way? Don't you care about her at all?"

"Of course I care," Tim said. "I —" He broke off, and Amy saw a sudden look of comprehension cross his face. "This isn't about Amy, is it, Lou?" he said suddenly. "This is about you."

Lou stared. "What? What are you talking about?"

"All this emotion," Tim said. "This overreaction to Amy riding. I was right. You're scared of horses, aren't you?"

"Don't be ridiculous!" Lou snapped.

Tim shook his head. "I think you are. Oh, Lou, don't let what happened to me affect your life like this. I know I was injured. I know there are risks involved with riding and being around horses — there are with a lot of things in life, but we have to take chances." His eyes searched hers. "You've got to face this fear, Lou. If you don't, you'll always live with a sense of what might have been."

"Got to!" Lou spat. "How dare you tell me what I've got to do! You lost the right to do that the day you abandoned me!" she said, turning on her heel and marching away.

There was a silence. Amy glanced at her father. His face was white. "I'd better go after her," he said.

"No," Amy said quickly. "Leave her to calm down."

Tim hesitated for a moment and then nodded. "Maybe that would be for the best." He looked at Amy. "But I'm right. This is all to do with fear of riding."

"I know," Amy said, remembering the look of terror in Lou's eyes as she had seen her on Feather. It had been just the same as the look on Mrs Newhart's face as she had run across the ring after Feather had reared with Jo. Tim was right. Lou was scared, even if she wouldn't admit it.

Tim sighed. "I shouldn't have said anything. I don't want to leave with things on a bad note between us."

"Just give her a little time," Amy said, hoping she was right. She patted the pony beside her. "Well, I guess I'd better put Feather back in his stall."

"What are you going to do about him?" Tim asked as he followed her down the yard.

"I don't know," Amy said, forcing her mind to focus on the issue of Feather. "I guess it's really Jo who needs the remedy, not him. Maybe I could try giving her something to help her nerves — some of the Bach Flower Remedies are good for dealing with anxiety. But I just can't see Mrs Newhart allowing Jo near Feather again, even if I tell her what's wrong."

"Is there anyone who could help Jo change her mom's mind?" Tim asked. "What about the uncle who bought Feather?"

"I could ring Jo and ask," Amy said, feeling a glimmer of hope.

"Why not ring now? I'll put Feather away," Tim said.

Amy went down to the kitchen. There was no sign of Lou anywhere. Picking up the telephone, Amy punched in the Newharts' number. As she listened to it ringing she wondered what she'd say if Mrs Newhart answered the phone, but to her relief, it was Jo who took the call. Amy quickly explained what she thought the reasons might be behind Feather misbehaving. "Are you sure he's only ever played up when your mom's been watching?" she asked.

"Oh, Amy!" Jo exclaimed. "I think you're right. Can you tell Mom and persuade her not to sell Feather?"

"I doubt she'll listen to me," Amy said. "But I was wondering if there's anyone else she'll listen to in your family. The uncle who bought Feather, maybe?"

"He's in Canada," Jo said. "On business, for the next three months. The only other person in the family who knows about horses is my gran. Maybe she'll speak to Mom." Jo sounded more hopeful than sure.

"I thought you said that she'd sold all her horses after the accident," Amy said.

"That's right," Jo admitted. "And she doesn't know about Feather. Mom thought it might upset her if she knew I had a horse. We never mention horses when we visit. She's been afraid of them since the accident."

"Well, I don't think she sounds like she'll help," Amy said.

"But she might," Jo said. "Will you try to speak to her, Amy?"

Amy hesitated. "I guess I could have a go," she said doubtfully.

"Oh, thank you!" Jo cried.

When Amy put the receiver down, she looked at the name and number that Jo had given her. Would this work? Taking a deep breath, she punched in the new number.

* * *

Ten minutes later, she put down the phone wondering whether she had done the right thing. Mary Butler, Jo's gran, had sounded very frail and it had taken Amy quite a long time to explain who she was and what she wanted. However, at last she had got the old lady to agree to come to Heartland and see Feather. Amy hoped that if Mrs Butler saw Jo riding him, then she would realize that he wasn't dangerous and would help persuade Mrs Newhart to let Jo keep him.

She rang Jo again. "Your gran's agreed to come and see him later this afternoon," she said.

"But that's brilliant!" Jo exclaimed.

"She hasn't said she'll help persuade your mom," Amy said, remembering how little Mrs Butler had said beyond agreeing, rather nervously, to come to Heartland that afternoon. "But at least she's coming. Can you come over about four o'clock to ride Feather?"

"I can't," Jo said. "Mom's banned me from getting on him again. Oh, Amy, what am I going to do?"

"OK, don't worry, Jo. We'll find a way of sorting this out," Amy said quickly, half-believing it herself.

After she got off the phone again, Amy set about finishing off the yard chores with her dad and Ben. She had hoped that an opportunity would come up for her dad to speak to Lou and sort things out. However, much to her concern, just before lunchtime, she saw Lou get into her car and drive away.

"Where's Lou gone?" she asked, bursting into the kitchen where Grandpa was sitting reading the local paper.

"Lunch with Scott," Grandpa replied.

"But it's Daddy's last day here!" Amy exclaimed.

"Yes, I thought it was a little odd," Grandpa said. "But she seemed determined to go." He saw Amy's face fall. "Has something happened?"

"Not really," Amy said, not wanting him to worry. "It's nothing." She went back on to the yard. Nothing. Daddy was leaving in three hours. What if Lou wasn't back by then?

Chapter Twelve

Three hours later, Lou still hadn't returned.

"Well, I have to go," Tim said to Amy. "I've got to pack and check out of the hotel."

"But you can't go without saying goodbye to Lou," Amy protested.

"Believe me, I don't want to," Tim said, looking at his watch. "But I haven't got much choice if I want to catch my plane home!"

Suddenly, there was the sound of a car coming up the drive. "It's Lou!" Amy exclaimed in relief.

It was. Lou parked and got out.

"Daddy's just leaving," Amy told her.

As she spoke, Grandpa came out of the house. "So you're going then?" he said to Tim.

"That's right, Jack," Tim replied. He looked awkwardly at Lou. "Lou…"

Lou marched to Jack's side. "Bye, Daddy," she said, her voice abrupt.

Amy saw her father glance at Jack and her heart sank. She knew there was no way he was going to get into a heavy talk with Lou with Grandpa standing there. Her thoughts raced as she tried to figure out a way of getting Grandpa out of the way for a few moments. But it was too late. Grandpa held out his hand.

"Goodbye, Tim," he said. "Thank you for coming. Truly."

Amy saw her dad's shoulders sag slightly. "Goodbye, Jack," he said, stepping forward to shake hands, and Amy knew then that he had given up hope of talking to Lou. "Thank you for allowing me to visit." He turned to Amy. "Bye, sweetheart," he said, hugging her tight. "Promise you'll come and stay with me sometime."

"I promise," Amy said, feeling tears springing to her eyes. After so long wishing that he wouldn't come and visit, she now didn't want to see him go, particularly not with everything feeling so unresolved. "And I'll phone and e-mail you."

Tim kissed her hair. "You'd better. After all, I want to know what happens when Mary Butler visits."

"Mary Butler?" Grandpa said.

"Jo's gran," Amy explained. "She's coming this afternoon. I'm hoping that if I can show her Feather's not dangerous –" she glanced at Lou who looked quickly away – "then she'll help me persuade Mrs Newhart to let Jo keep him." She saw

Grandpa raise his eyebrows. "I know it's a long shot but I've got to try something."

"I really hope it works," Tim said. He hugged her once more and then, letting her go, he turned to Lou.

"Lou?" he said holding out his hands. Lou's jaw clenched and for a moment, Amy thought she was going to ignore their father's outstretched hands. But then she walked briskly forwards. They hugged briefly, her body stiff. "Have a safe journey," she said.

Her voice was cool and polite, but there were signs of strain around her eyes and mouth, *Just say that you'll miss him, Lou*, Amy thought desperately. But Lou didn't. Moving back beside Grandpa, she watched as Tim got into his car and started the engine.

"Bye," he said, lowering the window. "Get in touch soon." Amy could see the sadness in his eyes and she felt a lump of tears in her throat. "Bye, Daddy," she said, swallowing hard.

He drove off.

For a moment no one spoke, and then Lou turned and ran into the house.

Amy went to go after her but Grandpa stopped her. "Lou's got some issues to deal with, Amy. She needs time on her own."

"I just don't get her," Amy said in frustration. "She didn't say she'd miss him or anything. She hardly even hugged him."

"I know," Jack said gently. "Maybe next time he visits things will be easier."

Next time, Amy thought, as he went back into the house. *But I don't want to wait until next time. Who knows when that will be?*

She kicked a loose stone. Feeling miserable, she walked up to Feather's stall to give him a last brush over before Jo's grandmother arrived.

At five minutes to four, a minivan came up the driveway. An old lady with silver hair was driving. As the old lady parked, Amy walked over, butterflies fluttering in her stomach. What was Mrs Butler going to be like? If her family never mentioned horses around her since the accident, was she really going to help? Amy groaned inwardly. Was this all just a huge mistake?

The door opened. "Hello," Amy said. "I'm Amy Fleming."

"Mary Butler," the old lady said, a nervous quaver to her voice. "Pleased to meet you." They shook hands. Mrs Butler looked just a few years older than Grandpa but very frail. "Would you be so kind as to help me get my wheelchair from out of the back?" she said, in a low, shaky voice

"Of course," Amy said. As she opened the back door, she noticed that the minivan was specially adapted. The back had no seats in, just Mrs Butler's wheelchair. She brought it out and helped Mrs Butler into it.

"Thank you," the old lady said. She looked around the yard and, for a moment, Amy had the impression that in her eyes was the look of a trapped animal who wanted to flee.

Amy's heart sank. This was a bad, bad idea. Mrs Butler was never going to be able to help. Just then, the back door opened and to Amy's surprise Lou came out. "Hello," she said, walking over to Mrs Butler. "I'm Lou Fleming, Amy's sister."

For one nightmare moment, Amy wondered whether Lou was about to launch into a speech about how dangerous Feather was. But she didn't. She just smiled. "Would you like to take a look around the place?"

Mary Butler hesitated and took a deep breath. "Yes. That would be nice," she whispered.

As Lou moved behind the wheelchair and took hold of the handles, Amy saw that her eyes were red. It looked as if she'd been crying. However, she couldn't question her sister at that moment. Lou seemed to be unaware of Amy's stare as she wheeled Jo's grandmother over to the turn-out paddocks and then up to stable block. She pointed out each of the horses in turn. Wondering why she was helping, Amy decided to follow her.

As Lou chatted about the horses, saying their names and a little about them, Jo's grandmother visibly seemed to relax. Seeing this, Amy stopped worrying about why Lou was helping and just felt relieved.

"This is Red and Rosie and Jake," Lou said pointing out each horse as she spoke. Red and Rosie were spooked by the wheelchair but Jake bent his great bay head and snuffled at Mrs Butler's hair.

"Jake! Manners!" Amy said, moving quickly to push the big horse back.

"It's ... it's OK," Mary Butler said. "I don't mind." With trembling fingers, she reached into her coat pocket and pulled out a mint. "Here, boy," she murmured, holding it out on the flat of her hand. "I think this is what you're looking for."

Always eager for treats, Jake gently lipped the sweet up. Jo's grandmother sat as if transfixed. Crunching happily, Jake lifted his muzzle to her face and the old lady stroked his nose with her hand.

"Thirty years," she said, her voice so low that Amy almost didn't catch it. She glanced round at Amy and Lou. "This is the first time I've touched a horse in thirty years."

Even Lou seemed lost for words at this revelation.

"I take it you know about my accident?" Mary Butler said.

Amy and Lou nodded.

"And so you know that after it, I let all my horses be sold? My four beautiful horses."

Amy frowned at the word "let". "But I thought you wanted to sell them."

Mrs Butler shook her grey head. "Every time my husband or my daughter even looked at a horse I knew they were reminded of what they no longer had — a healthy wife, a strong mother."

"So you gave up your horses?" Lou said.

The old lady nodded. "I got rid of everything to do with horses — the stables were turned into a garage, my horse pictures and trophies were thrown away, even my jodhpurs were burned."

Amy was stunned. If she'd have known that Jo's grandmother had put such a distance between herself and horses, she'd never have called her.

Lou looked curious. "So, why did you agree to come here today, then?"

"I don't know," Mrs Butler said. "I think it was just the push I needed. My husband – Jo-Ann's grandfather – died last year, and since then I've been wondering whether what I did was right or misguided." She reached out to touch Jake's nose again. "And now I know," she said. "Seeing these horses, smelling them, touching them. How could I have shut all these sensations from my life? I made a big mistake – a terrible mistake." Her voice shook on the last word. "For thirty years, I've denied something that could have given me so much happiness. How stupid I was."

Amy glanced at Lou, and saw that her sister's face looked thoughtful.

The old lady shook her head. "I don't want Jo-Ann to suffer in the same way. Now, where is her pony? I want to see him."

"He's in the back barn," Amy said.

Lou didn't say a word as she pushed the wheelchair up to the barn.

"So you're the fella who's been causing all sorts of trouble?" Mrs Butler said when they introduced her to Feather. "You're certainly a handsome boy."

"Gran!" They all turned. Jo was running down the aisle towards them.

"What are you doing here, Jo?" Amy said.

"I know I can't ride Feather," Jo said breathlessly. "But I had to see my gran and tell her how awesome my pony is. I wrote Mom a note saying I'd come to collect my jacket and I'd be back soon. Please, Gran," she said, stopping by her grandmother's chair. "You've got to help. Feather's not dangerous." She suddenly seemed to notice that the old lady was patting Feather's neck. "Aren't you afraid of him?" she exclaimed.

"I've never been afraid of a horse in my life, honey," Mary Butler said, smiling. "I've just kept away from them. But I'm beginning to realize how much I have lost." She took Jo's hand. "And I don't want to see you miss out in the same way. Let me watch you ride your pony and if he is safe, like Amy says, then I'll do everything in my power to persuade your mom to let you keep him."

"Oh, Gran, thank you!" Jo gasped. She looked worried. "But Mom said I wasn't to ride him."

Mrs Butler squeezed her hand. "Don't worry. I'll take the blame."

Ten minutes later, Feather was tacked up. "Now, before you get on, take a few drops of this on your tongue," Amy said, handing Jo a small brown bottle.

"What is it?" Jo peered at the label. "Agrimony? What's that?"

154

"It's a Bach Flower Remedy," Amy explained. "It releases any tension you're feeling and it'll help you to relax."

Jo took the remedy and then led Feather up to the school. Amy joined Lou and Mrs Butler at the gate.

"Just stay calm," Amy told Jo as she mounted.

"I will," Jo said. And she did. Whether it was the remedy, or the fact that she knew why Feather had been misbehaving, or that she had her grandmother's support, Amy couldn't tell. All that mattered was that Jo relaxed into the saddle and Feather behaved like a dream.

"See, Gran!" Jo said triumphantly as she finally brought him to a stop by the gate. "Isn't he perfect?"

"He is," Mary Butler said quietly. She turned to Amy. "You know, you're a very remarkable young woman. To work out what was wrong with this pony and then to go to the lengths of contacting me. Thank you."

"So will you try to persuade Mom to let me keep him, Gran?" Jo asked.

Her grandmother nodded. "Most certainly I will." The pinched look had left her face and a happy flush of colour now suffused her cheekbones. "And I'll also tell her that I intend to start to ride again myself." She smiled. "I may be seventy, but there's still a good few years left in me, and I want to make up for lost time."

Jo's face lit up. "But Gran, that's fantastic! We could go riding together." She patted Feather's neck. "Oh, Feather, do you hear that – isn't it the best news?"

"Jo-Ann!" The half-scream, half-shout made them all swing round.

There on the path was Mrs Newhart, coming towards them. She was staring at Jo and Feather with shock in her eyes.

Chapter Thirteen

"What on earth do you think you are doing, Jo?" Mrs Newhart cried, her face paling. She started to run towards them. "I saw your note and knew you'd be doing something like this. Thank goodness I came. Get off that pony right now!"

"Donna, stop it!"

Mrs Newhart stopped in her tracks and, for the first time, her gaze took in the old lady in the wheelchair, half-hidden behind Lou and Amy. "Mom?" she said in astonishment. "What are you doing here?"

"I'm here because Amy rang me up and told me about Jo-Ann's pony." Mrs Butler looked at Jo. "Maybe you'd better dismount for a moment, Jo, while we explain things to your mom." As Jo dismounted, Mrs Butler shook her head. "Why didn't you tell me what was happening, Donna?" she said to Mrs Newhart.

Mrs Newhart's eyes flickered from Mrs Butler to Jo. She looked as if she didn't know what to do first – tell Jo off or answer Mrs Butler's question.

"You should have told me about Feather," Mrs Butler said to her.

"I ... I didn't want to upset you, Mother," Mrs Newhart said. "I know how much you hate horses."

"Hate them?" Mrs Butler said. "I've never hated a thing in my life, Donna. I gave horses up because I didn't want to upset you and your father."

"So, you're not scared of them?" Mrs Newhart said falteringly.

"No," Mrs Butler replied. "Not at all."

"But even after everything that happened? The horse falling on you?"

"It was an accident," Mrs Butler said. "The horse wasn't to blame, Donna. It no more meant it to happen than I did." She sighed. "I know how much it affected you, but please, don't let it blight Jo-Ann's life too. Protect her, yes – but not at the expense of her happiness. Feather isn't a dangerous pony. I've been watching him. He and Jo have a wonderful bond. Let her keep him."

Mrs Newhart looked lost for words.

Lou quickly spoke up. "Your mother's right, Mrs Newhart," she said. "Jo loves riding, and if you try and stop her doing it then she'll always have a sense of what might have been. Yes, there are risks, but there are risks in anything in life that's worthwhile."

Amy stared as she recognized their father's words from earlier. But Lou avoided her sister's gaze.

Mrs Newhart nodded slowly. "You're right," she sighed. "I know you are. But..." Her eyes glanced anxiously at Feather. "Is he really safe? I mean, earlier, when he reared..."

"Amy can explain his behaviour," Mrs Butler said. She looked at Amy, who quickly took her cue and explained why Feather had been playing up.

"I see," Mrs Newhart said slowly, as Amy finished. "So it was because Feather was trying to protect Jo. He could tell she wasn't happy?"

"Yes," Amy said, nodding. "He's a very sensitive pony and he loves Jo very much."

"Please can I keep him, Mom?" Jo burst out.

Mrs Newhart took a deep breath. "All right, Jo-Ann," she said. "I want you to be happy. Yes, you can keep him."

"Oh, Mom!" Jo cried. Flinging the reins at Amy she raced across the sand and threw her arms round her mom. "Thank you! Thank you so much!"

Half an hour later, Jo, her mom and Mrs Butler left, with Jo chatting happily about how she was going to help her gran learn to ride again.

"I've never seen Jo so happy," Amy said, as she and Lou waved them off.

"I'm really pleased for her," Lou said quietly. "And for

Feather." She wandered over to the nearby paddock fence and leaned against it with a sigh.

"What's up?" Amy said, joining her.

"I had some news this morning," Lou said. She looked across the paddock. The evening shadows were just starting to lengthen across the grass and the last rays of the sun fell on the grazing shapes of Dancer and Solo. "I've been trying to find the right moment to tell you – we didn't get the land."

"We didn't?" Amy said, frowning. "So who did? Green Briar?"

"No, don't worry," Lou answered her quickly. "The Youngs have decided not to sell."

"Not to sell?" Amy looked puzzled. "You mean they've pulled out of the deal?"

"Yeah, they're going to extend their farm and try and make a go of things for themselves instead." Lou shrugged.

"Oh, Lou." Amy touched her sister's arm sympathetically. "I'm sorry. I know it meant a lot to you."

Lou stared out at the horses for a moment. "It did," she admitted. "But I've been thinking about it since lunchtime, and I think it might be for the best. If I'm honest, I guess I wanted it to happen so much, not because it would be the ideal thing for Heartland, but because I hoped it would make me feel more important. It would have been my very own project – something for me to work on and to shape." She glanced at Amy. "You, Grandpa, Ty – you all have your own roles here. I don't."

"But you do!" Amy protested in astonishment. "We couldn't run the business side of things without you."

"You could," Lou said sadly. "You could get someone else to do the accounts and marketing. You could hire an administrator."

"But they wouldn't have your ideas," Amy told her. "And, anyway, it's not just the business side of things that we need you for. You're good at talking to people – much better than I am, than any of us are. You were the one who persuaded Mrs Newhart to let Feather come to Heartland in the first place and this afternoon you were the one who made Mrs Butler feel at ease, and helped make Mrs Newhart understand why Jo should be allowed to keep Feather."

Lou looked slightly surprised. "I did?"

"Yes!" A question that had been lurking at the back of Amy's mind, rose to her lips. "Though what I don't get is why you came out to help when Mrs Butler arrived. I mean, this morning you'd made it pretty clear that you thought Feather was dangerous."

"I know." Lou hesitated. "But I ... I talked that over with Scott at lunchtime and he felt that Daddy wouldn't have let you ride Feather if he'd thought that the horse was dangerous. He made me realize that I'd overreacted."

"So why didn't you say anything to Daddy before he left?" Amy said, frowning. "He was really upset, Lou."

Lou didn't reply.

"Lou," Amy said, remembering the hurt in their father's

eyes as he'd left. "You should have said something. You should have talked to him. He didn't want to leave things on such a bad note with you. He wanted to sort things out. He…"

The words *loves you* froze on her lips as she saw Lou's shoulders suddenly shake.

"Oh, Amy!" The words burst from Lou in a sob. "I so wanted to. I know I should have made up. But I felt so mad at him, I just couldn't do it."

"But why?" Amy said, bewildered.

"Why?" Lou turning on her. "Why do you think? All week it's been you and Daddy doing this, you and Daddy doing that. Well, what about me?"

Amy stared. "You could have done things with Daddy too, but you didn't want to. You just kept working inside."

"He could have come in and seen me."

"But you kept saying you were busy!" Amy exclaimed. "Lou, you can't blame him for not disturbing you when you told him you were working. That's not fair!"

"I know, I know." Lou bowed her head. "I'm sorry," she said quietly. "It wasn't your fault, Amy — or Daddy's. It was mine. I just had this whole big idea in my head of what Daddy's visit would be like — you know, running up the drive and throwing my arms around him. All that soppy stuff that you see in films. But it wasn't like that. Daddy's changed so much."

Amy hesitated. "Are you sure it's Daddy who's changed, Lou?" she said tentatively. "Not you? After all," she paused, wondering how to put her thoughts into words without offending Lou, "not liking horses any more is quite a major difference."

"It's not that I don't like them," Lou said. "It's just ... just..."

Amy wanted to finish Lou's sentence but something told her that the words had to come from her sister. "Just what?" she prompted.

"I'm scared of them," Lou whispered. She swallowed, her eyes meeting Amy's. "Daddy was right. I am afraid. Oh, I don't mind handling them," she said, seeing Amy's expression. "It's just riding them. Whenever I think about getting on one all I can see in my mind is the picture of Daddy falling and Pegasus crumpling on the floor." Fresh sobs tore through her. "I was there that night. I watched it happen and I've never forgotten it. That's why I avoided Daddy. He knew, and I couldn't face him. He's always been so brave. I couldn't bear it if he thought me a coward."

Amy touched her sister's back. "It's OK," she murmured. "It'll be all right, Lou."

Lou raised her tear-streaked face. "How?" she demanded. "You can't change the past."

"No, but we can move on," Amy said. "Remember what Daddy said – you can't let what happened to him ruin your life, but if you don't face your fears it will. You can't shut horses out of your life – not when you used to love them so much. You saw how much Jo's grandmother regretted it."

"I know," Lou whispered. "But, Amy, I just can't get on one — I can't."

Amy thought quickly. If she was dealing with a frightened horse, what would she do? *Take things slowly of course*, she thought. *One step at a time.*

"So don't start by riding," she said. "Just start working one from the ground." An idea grew in her mind. "Join-up, Lou. You could try to join-up with one of the horses."

"No, it wouldn't work—" Lou began, shaking her head.

"Yes, it would," Amy insisted. She glanced out of the barn door. It was dusk, but not quite evening yet. "You could do it now, Lou."

"Now?" Lou echoed.

"Yes, with —" Amy thought quickly. "With Sugarfoot," she said.

Ten minutes later, Lou was reluctantly standing in the middle of the circular ring with Amy. "I'm really not sure about this," she said.

"You'll be fine," Amy said, wishing she could give some of her own confidence to Lou. She unclipped the little Shetland's lead-rope and patted his chestnut back. "He hasn't joined-up with anyone before, but I'm sure he'll be perfect."

Looking rather surprised to be up in the ring, Sugarfoot wandered away, his muzzle to the sand, his thick flaxen mane flopping over his neck. "Just remember, keep your shoulders square and your eyes on his," Amy said, starting to go towards the gate.

"Aren't you going to stay with me?" Lou asked anxiously.

"You'll find it harder if I'm there," Amy said. "You need to just concentrate on Sugarfoot, listen to the signals he's giving you and respond to them."

She climbed over the gate. The sun had dropped below the horizon and the shadows around the ring were lengthening. In the tall trees behind the ring, a single bird sang softly in the evening light. Amy leaned against the gate, her eyes on her sister. Lou was standing in the centre of the ring, moving the rope rather nervously from hand to hand.

It took all of Amy's willpower not to shout out an instruction. But she knew that this was something Lou had to figure out on her own.

Rather awkwardly, Lou flicked the end of the long-line towards Sugarfoot. He looked at her in surprise and trotted a few paces before slowing again and stopping to snuff at the floor. She clicked her tongue and pitched the rope at his hindquarters. Sugarfoot swung round and looked at her.

Amy gripped the gate. "Eyes, Lou, eyes!" she muttered.

As if she had heard, Lou fixed her eyes on the chestnut Shetland and squared her shoulders with his. This time, when she pitched the rope, Sugarfoot broke into a trot, and then, as Lou moved the rope towards him again, into a canter, his short legs pounding round the ring.

Seeming to grow in confidence with every circuit he made, Lou kept him going, working him round the ring, changing direction, sending him on again.

"There!" Amy whispered as Sugarfoot made the tiniest movement with his mouth. Soon he was chewing and licking and his head started stretching down. Amy glanced at Lou's face. It was utterly focused on the little Shetland. Suddenly she turned her shoulders in. Sugarfoot stopped within a few strides, and then, with hardly a hesitation, walked straight across the ring to where Lou was standing, her eyes on the ground, her back to him. With a snort he stopped behind her and nuzzled her back.

"Way to go, Lou!" Amy whispered, smiling broadly as Lou turned to the pony and rubbed his forehead, just as Amy herself would have done.

Remembering to walk away, Lou set off across the ring. Sugarfoot walked after her. Wherever Lou went, the little Shetland followed like a shadow. At last Lou stopped.

"Lou! You did it!" Amy cried, unable to contain her delight any longer.

Lou's face lit up with an ecstatic grin as Amy scrambled over the gate. "I did! I really did!"

As Amy reached her, she flung her arms round Amy and they hugged each other. When Lou drew back her eyes were shining. "Oh, Amy, it was the most wonderful, amazing thing!"

"I know," Amy said, grinning.

Lou's face glowed. It was as if all her earlier tension and

unhappiness had been completely wiped away. "It felt like magic! The feeling I got when he came up to me." Her voice bubbled over with emotion. "It was like electricity. Suddenly I felt I could..."

"Speak his language," Amy said.

Lou nodded. "That's it exactly!" She ran a hand through her hair. "Oh, wow!" she said, grinning from ear to ear. "I almost feel I could get on a horse and ride right now."

"That's for another day," Amy said, knowing how important it was to just take one day at a time.

Lou nodded. "Yes, you're right." She patted Sugarfoot and grinned joyfully at Amy. "Oh, wow. I don't think I'm ever going to come down to earth."

A familiar male voice called through the growing darkness, "Why try?"

Amy and Lou swung round.

"Daddy!" they both gasped, staring at their father who had stepped out of the shadows at the side of the ring.

"I couldn't leave things as they were," Tim said, opening the gate and coming towards them across the ring. "I was on my way to the airport when I decided to stop by. I called at the house and Jack said you were both up here."

"So did you see Lou joining-up?" Amy asked eagerly.

"I certainly did," Tim smiled. "I saw it all."

"You were right, Daddy," Lou said. "I was scared."

"And what about now?" Tim asked, watching her closely

"Not so much," Lou said. "And maybe," she took a deep

breath, "maybe when you visit next time, perhaps I won't be scared at all."

"Lou, I'm so proud of you," Tim said softly. "I know how hard it is to face up to your fears. I was so afraid of getting in contact with you both again and so I put it off again and again. It was only your persistence that made me get in touch. I lost twelve years of your lives, but it could have been so many more."

Lou looked a bit embarrassed. "I wish I had spent more time with you this week."

"It's OK," Tim said. "I know it was hard. We've all had some adjusting to do. At first I didn't know what to say when I saw you – my little girl, grown into a confident successful young woman with a life and career of her own."

"And a fear of horses," Lou put in.

Tim shook his head. "I never meant to upset you about that. I just couldn't bear the thought of you wasting years of your life by giving into your fear – doing what I did, basically. I just wanted you to be happy – that's all I've ever wanted for both of you." He looked from Amy to Lou. "I know I can't take back the pain I've caused you in the past. But I want you to know that if you ever need me, I'll be here for you. I accept that after everything I've done, I've lost the right to call myself your father, but I would really like it –" he paused – "if we could be friends."

"You'll always be more than that to us," Amy said, going over to hug him.

Lou followed her. "Amy's right. "You're our daddy, and nothing can ever change that."

Amy saw the emotion in her father's eyes as he gathered them both into his arms. "My daughters," he murmured into their hair. "My two wonderful daughters."

They hugged for a further moment and then Lou pulled back.

"There's something else I need to tell you, Daddy," she said. "It's about the land – we didn't get it. There isn't going to be a riding school."

"Oh, Lou, I'm sorry," Tim said, looking at her sympathetically. "I know how much you wanted it."

"It's OK," Lou answered. "I'm not sure I wanted it for the right reasons. I think I just wanted to feel important." She glanced at Amy. "But Amy's made me realize that I *am* important here at Heartland – I do belong. And if we need to think of a way to raise more funds, well," she grinned. "I'm never short of money-making ideas."

"That's my girl," Tim said. "And I want to hear all about your plans next time we meet up. But right now," he added reluctantly, "I'm going to have to go or I'll miss my plane. We'll see each other again soon?" He made it into a question.

Lou smiled through her tears. "You don't think that after all the trouble I went to track you down I'm going to let you lose touch with us again, do you?"

Amy grinned. "You'll have go much further than Australia if you want to escape from Lou, Daddy."

"Heck!" Tim said with a mock-frown. "And I thought I was safe over there." He smiled at Amy. "Don't you stop taking risks, you hear."

"I don't think there's any danger of that," Lou said wryly.

"And next time I see you," Tim said, turning to her, "maybe we'll all go out on the trails together."

Lou smiled. "I'd like that more than anything else in the world."

Looking at her sister's face, Amy suddenly remembered the old photograph of Lou sitting on her pony. Joyful, delighted – just as she had been in the photo – Lou seemed a very different person to the one Amy had comforted in the barn just a short time ago.

"I'd better go," Tim said. "And just remember, Lou. You are needed and you do belong – here at Heartland, and with me and Amy too."

He kissed them both on the forehead, patted Feather and then, with one last look, the tall figure disappeared into the darkness.

"It's getting late," Lou said softly, as the night closed around them. "We should go in."

Sugarfoot snorted. As Amy moved to pat him, she saw her sister's hand lift too.

Their eyes met. Lou smiled and stroked Sugarfoot's neck. "You know, I think we're a family again, Amy – a real family."